The Pig Plantagenet

'Now,' said the wild boar, Grondin, Plantagenet's cousin. 'I suppose you've come to ask about your father.'

'How did you know that?' gasped the pig.

'Everyone asks about his father sooner or later.'

'It's just that I'm so different.'

'Different from whom?'

'I don't know. From you, anyway.'

'Does it matter?'

'I'm not so strong as you. Not so hardy. Not so independent.'

'Does that matter?'

'It matters to me.'

'What's the point of being strong, hardy, independent when you live on a farm with a pretty girl making a silk purse out of your ear and her father stuffing you with – did you really say ten per cent white-fish meal?'

'I should never have accepted the farm if I hadn't been . . . ' Plantagenet hesitated.

'Handicapped? Strange? Illegitimate?' questioned Grondin remorselessly.

'Different,' said the little pig stolidly.

ALLEN ANDREWS
The Pig Plantagenet

ARROW BOOKS

Written for
Xavier & Caroline

Arrow Books Limited
17–21 Conway Street, LondonW1P 6JD.

An imprint of the Hutchinson Publishing Group

London Melbourne Sydney Auckland
Johannesburg and agencies
throughout the world

First published by Hutchinson 1980

Arrow edition 1982

The author pays tribute to the inspiration of
Michel Héloin's manuscript, *Le Roman de Fulbert*

Text © Allen Andrews 1980

Set in Monotype Goudy

Made and printed in Great Britain
by The Anchor Press Ltd
Tiptree Essex

ISBN 0 09 927870 7

Contents

1

All Creatures Here Below

Bafrin, the falcon, flew straight and steep. He had a fancy to go up so fast and sheer that he would do without the long glides he usually treated himself to between volleys of rapid wing-beats. He saved it all up until he had got to the top of the airy incline he had set himself for morning exercise and a good view. Then he soared in supreme indulgence, as dreamily and gluttonously as a Duchess of Aquitaine at a love-feast. Poitou lay beneath him.

Most of the country was forest. Dominating the living map spread out below, its dark mass lay like an ink blot capriciously smeared on parchment by a conqueror. But there were signs that shrewd forces had challenged the ancient régime, with stone and locks and keys. One green-and-grey keyhole, inset on the edge of the black, marked the castle of Crespin and its manorial lands. A brown blur, not so sharply scythed, but rather chewed out of the forest boundary, was the isolated farm of La Tranchée. Far to the north, where Bafrin rarely hovered, the sable forest thinned and bowed and scraped to make room for a river which washed a yellow town.

Steady flashes of silver light glinted up to Bafrin's eye from a courtyard inside Crespin. Something unnaturally regular, measured and menacing, was going on there, and had been noticeable for many days now. The heavily forti-fied castle had a moat surrounding a towered and turreted curtain wall which in turn protected several courtyards and the central kernel of the square stone keep, cornered from undercroft to battlements by circular stairways which camouflaged the beautiful inner lines of the high great hall and the lord's apartments leading from its gallery. Outside the main castle gates, beyond the drawbridge, lay the straight village street with houses backing on to the two huge fields, one each side of the street, which provided the only culti-vated land. It was a pleasant expanse, but from where Bafrin soared the space of the castle and the village and the fields was a mere morsel of habitable land scooped out of the dark forest and connected with other remote human habitations by a thin forest ride traced timidly through the boundary timber.

Much smaller than the dingle claimed by the castle was the dell of the outlying forest farm of La Tranchée. Its high dry-stone wall and protective moat around the house and stables were at one point within a few yards of the thick woods from which the farm had been cut. But on the other side of the estate greenwood merged into underwood, underwood to brushwood, brushwood to open clearings and on to the marshy side of a stream. The farm stood with its back to the forest but had the relief of an open prospect to the south.

The girl Adèle gazed at the pig Plantagenet from the open door of his spotless sty in the farmyard of La Tranchée, and the pig regarded the girl with just as deep attention. Adèle slightly raised her head and said, not at all in a religious voice but as if she knew who she was talking to: 'Praise to thee, my Lord, for all thy creatures, Brother Sun and Sister Moon, Brother Wind and Sister Water, Brother Fire and Mother Earth, and my brother the pig Plantagenet.' She leaned and kneaded the flesh of his shoulders a little. Plantagenet let her roll his neck with the greatest good humour, although he shot like a crossbow-bolt beneath the straw of his litter at the mere lifting of anyone else's fingers. 'She is the only one in all the farm,' he told himself, 'who does not prod me to see how thick the fat will be beneath the crackling. Praise the Lord for my sister Adèle.'

Plantagenet did not speak in Adèle's language, but in his own, which was very fluent, like thought, and is used by all animals. He understood Adèle's language perfectly when she spoke to him, but not so well when she spoke to others. He understood Adèle's father, Maister Brémand, fairly clearly when he spoke to him, because Maister Brémand had rather a weakness for Plantagenet. Most domestic animals understood people who loved or hated them, but for the rest, beyond an odd word it was all pretty much rhubarb. The free animals recognized and sometimes playfully imitated a surprising number of human words, but they were all very coarse expressions and strictly unrepeatable, except in innocence. For the animals of the forest mainly encountered humans hallooing and swearing with weapons in their hands. They classified them as unpredictably wild animals who never stopped roaring, and indulgently called them mandrakes, after the two-legged poisonous plants which shriek as they are pulled out of the ground.

Plantagenet abandoned himself to the pleasant fondling from Adèle's firm milkmaid fingers. He was a little absent-minded, and was not sure whether he had actually praised the Lord for her or only thought of it, since the two communions were so alike. Being no miser, he said again, 'Praise the Lord for my sister Adèle.'

A single sound came down from heaven, like a hoarse despairing hiccup. Plantagenet did not bother to look up into the washed blue sky. He could never see what he had heard, and it made his eyes water trying. Clearly one of the

falcons was encouraging himself with a small personal insult
before beginning a burst of power. At a guess it would be
Bafrin the Noble.

Bafrin beat hard and exhilaratingly in full positive lift,
then soared with an occasional trim of his primaries to keep
within the thermal. The glittering flashes caught his eye
again. He focussed his attention on the castle of Crespin
and saw on the sunny side of an inner bailey a squad of
mandrakes rhythmically pulling and pushing long branches
with shining ends, first up and down, then forward and
backward, with a solitary mandrake standing in front of
them apparently doing nothing except to howl at the others.
All the mandrakes were screaming as if they had just been
plucked out of the ground, but there were two sorts of
shrieks. The big crowd who were endlessly pushing and
pulling the gleaming branches were probably at the point of
death or deep exhaustion, Bafrin speculated, although they
seemed young with the attractive gawkiness of bear cubs.
Realizing that this was their doom, they must be drawing on
the elemental strength of their whole flock to unite in some
prayer or assertion of flock-immortality that would carry
them through the shadow. Their sombre chorus rose up in a
steady and entirely hopeless chant which came to Bafrin's
ear as, 'One two three four, pike up pike down, five six
seven eight, pike in pike out.' The notably wizened mandrake in front of these doomed creatures had a howl which
was not only far more high and piercing, but ululated
exactly four times as fast as the groans of the sacrificial
victims, so that with each of their movements there was a
quick, shrill side-drum tattoo which sounded to Bafrin like,
'IN to his guts, TWIST in his guts, OUT with his guts,' and on
every fourth movement it accelerated into a triple-time
ruffle of, 'Orrible orrible orrible enemy.' Occasionally the
solitary shrivelled mandrake spat the last ruffle personally
into the face of one of the sweating oblations, directing a

drumfire of abuse that was plainly lethal, for the clear face did not youthfully blush, but became knotted with the congestion caused by internal injury.

Bafrin wasted no more time trying to understand the incomprehensible, and circled over the forest. The trees were getting thin on top. With luck a silly wood-pigeon might expose itself. Some creatures seemed so deplorably dim that it was as much duty as delight to take them for dinner. It taught their survivors sound ecological sense. Look at that grazing sheep, drifting with every dreamy nibble towards the terrain of Hurlaud the wolf.

The shrivelled mandrake in the castle stealthily climbed a circular stairway to the battlements, flashing an eye through every fourth peep-hole to make sure his inferiors were still sweating while they could not see him. From the platform he, too, spared a glance at the forest. The very sight seemed to give him a convulsion, and he swung round instinctively to swear at the creatures he could unquestionably control.

The sombre forest was a remote world of its own. Its lords were the animals. Humans passed through it with difficulty and never felt at ease. It was a cool jungle where, beneath the tall trees, erectile undergrowth fixed its bayonets and deployed as quickset hedge, fallen boughs formed cross-barred gates and brambles fashioned mantraps, to ban, bar, tease and tangle men who ventured the passage. Horsemen never attempted its depths. Footmen armed themselves with axe and bill-hook, and preferably with archers and spearmen to cover them while they hacked. For they feared the lords of the forest who might emerge in anger. They feared them superstitiously, not reasonably or familiarly. So they did not know the proper names of the creatures they feared, though these were common gossip among the more alert of their domestic animals.

In his den in the Bel Air section of the forest, well furnished with rugs and draperies of moss and bracken,

Hurlaud the wolf pondered without too much anxiety on
the normal problems of the season. Neatly ranged in the
lair, his family slept peacefully around him, except that
Grand-Gueule was only pretending, for he thought it was
up to him to take over guard duty and let his father get his
head down. Hurlaud's yellow eyes, with the peculiar slant
of the squared pupils, having summed up the state of
consciousness of Grand-Gueule in an instant, were alert but
not unduly troubled. He was in good form, as fit as ever, the
undisputed leader of the pack whenever it formed, but
recognized by merit rather than birth – he was of good
family but his ranking name of Hurlaud of the Great Woods
had been earned personally in the field: however, he seldom
used his title.

He surveyed his family group around him. Young Braille,
Grand-Gueule and Voreau were some eighteen months old
now and after this winter they would doubtless push out on
their own, the young rips, one glorious year of bachelor
freedom, but that was the way of the world, and after that
they'd know what life was all about; and as for himself and
Dame Pernale there would be the responsibility of more
cubs in May. The babies Aube and Barthus were approaching six months. Really one shouldn't regard them as infants
any more. Within a week or two they would be out in the
open learning to hunt under the careful guidance of himself
and Dame Pernale – Hurlaud was always very formal when
he referred to his wife, even in his thoughts. From the condition of the berries he judged that it was not going to be an
easy winter, and pack-hunting would have to be organized
with stricter discipline than in the soft times of last year.
And that did not exclude attention to the wilfulness of his
own sons, particularly Grand-Gueule. No fear no favour,
but all the same one had to remember that the leaders of
tomorrow are often rather truculent in their youth. They
must not be crushed too severely. Fathers always tend to go

to extremes, either in nagging or indulgence. Perhaps he should have a word with his brother Baclin, the deputy leader of the pack.

Hurlaud mused into mid-afternoon and then took a nap before hunting. In the courtyard of the castle of Crespin the young soldiers slogged on at promoting their nervous breakdowns. In the farmyard at La Tranchée the pig Plantagenet snuggled comfortably into thinking about Adèle, and was jolted uncomfortably into thinking about other humans who never stopped prodding him for crackling, and about certain animals, including Hurlaud of the Great Woods, who cared nothing for crackling but fancied him raw. For Plantagenet was, through the accident of birth and adoption, a pioneer loner who ranged through three spheres of living, from the centre point of his clean straw bed to the surround of the mundane bustle of the farmyard and on to the humming outer space of the boundless forest beyond, where he had strong attachments and mighty fears – just as he had in bed. Like every frontiersman he had to make difficult adjustments to accept what he found. Plantagenet, a social character with the predictable yearning to *belong*, had to reckon with and reconcile the simplicity of the heart's affections, the complexity of human environment, and the inevitability of the survival of the fittest. They are problems which a more cautious Creator might have held his hand from presenting to an artless pig, and a sinfully imperfect pig at that – not very dutiful, meek only when frightened, over-delighting in revenge.

But even when Plantagenet was at his most dispirited he took courage from the possession of one grace which might be his salvation. Adèle assured him he was almost godly with it. He was a clean pig. He liked living clean, he claimed no particular virtue from it, that was how he was made and he suspected that there was a deal of double talk about the whole subject. Sometimes the local lepers, on the way from

their lazar-house to the hole in the wall of the church where
they were allowed to see the Elevation, passed Plantagenet
ringing their cracked bells with doleful cries of, 'Unclean!
Unclean!' Plantagenet often wanted to join them with a
label round his neck, written in Adèle's best script and
signed by the lord of the manor, proclaiming, 'Very clean!
Very clean!' Then he planned to nudge them companionably, to show that he didn't think he was any cleaner than
they were, and anyway he knew how rarely they were
infectious. But the only time he tried this he was naturally
not wearing a label, and the lepers kicked him away and
called him a dirty pig. Heigh-ho. Perhaps it would be
simpler to abandon his pretensions as an avant-garde philo-
sopher and accept domestic status. He looked around him.
Apart from the crackling problem – and his dissident
scepticism was at least coping with that – domesticity had
its attractions. He gazed appreciatively at the good order of
La Tranchée.

The farm was a large solid stone building in the shape of
an H. The dwelling-house of the Brémands was on the cross-
stroke of the H looking out on the main courtyard. To the
left of the principal apartments there were the domestic
servants' quarters, and on the right were the dormitories
laid out for the regular farm labourers and the journeymen
who were bound to give so many days' work a year. Some
of them had land, or were waiting for land, at La Tranchée
or elsewhere.

The building which formed one entire long down-stroke
of the H was made up of cattle-stalls, stables and sheepfolds.
The other long shaft of the H building was given over to
barns, grain-stores and fodder-housing. The rear courtyard
was cluttered with tumbrils, wagons, carts, brakes and all
the cultivating tools. Its square shape was broken by a
newly-built annexe containing the fowlhouses, the adjoining
pig-sty, and a spacious barn.

The whole complex was protected by a dry-stone wall some ten feet high. A drawbridge was operated from a strong gate-house which opened on to the main courtyard opposite Maister Brémand's house. Every night the heavy ironclad oak doors of this porch were carefully closed. Outside the wall was a wide moat high with water. For the forest was not a stone's throw from a sector of the wall, and there were seasons when the forest animals were hungry. Although less could be done against the strong-swimming foxes, the best general protection was the hazard of the brimming ditch.

The home farm was clean and tidy, the walls were whitened with lime, the main courtyard was cobbled with stones, and the cracks were regularly weeded. The poultry – chickens, geese, ducks, guineafowl – frolicked there at their ease.

Defence as well as the daily labour was provided by six regular farm workers and three journeymen. Two domestic servants, very pretty in their persons and very efficient in their tasks, managed the housekeeping and prepared the meals. Four guard dogs completed the security forces, the most menacing being a fierce mastiff named Hargneu. There was also the beagle Rupert, who had a special relationship with his master.

Maister Brémand, with the help of his wife Madame Matilda, and of his only surviving child Adèle, ran this little world. People remembered that there had been a son and heir, a boy whom everyone loved, but even before his voice had broken he had taken the Cross and gone on a hopeless Crusade amid a great rout of deluded children, and he was missing, presumed dead. Although her parents on rare occasions went into storms of passionate anger about the loss of their son, Adèle was not bitter, for she followed Little Brother Francis, who was not then a saint, in looking with as much love as possible on man and beast, friend and foe, victim and deceiver.

Maister Brémand was rather surly, as is often the case with people who are ranged for life against that tough adversary, the land. Madame Matilda was masterful enough at home and – as wagging tongues whispered in the village and the town – took that manner to the point of bossiness outside. But as far as the servants in the house and on the farm were concerned the Brémands were fair and decent masters. Open-hearted young Adèle, who helped her mother in supervising the housekeeping, treated everyone as a friend and charmed them all with her laughing high spirits. She was responsible for the good humour in the house and her parents saw to the good living. For they lived well. The cellars overflowed with noble wines of which Maister Brémand was very proud, and the pantries were crammed with fine food – prime hams, pâtés, eggs and every kind of flour. Maister Brémand farmed well and prosperously, and the excellent condition in which he maintained the land earned him many compliments from his lord, Messire de Frébois, who lost no opportunity to down a pint of his tenant's best wine on the way home from a day's hunting. That esteem compensated Brémand for whatever pinpricks of jealousy he experienced from other quarters.

The pig Plantagenet lived in the rear courtyard, in the pig-sty built in the new annexe.

Plantagenet had arrived at La Tranchée four years previously as a plump pink sucking-pig, a present from Maister Brémand's brother as a reward for some service rendered. There was a mystery about his birth. He was a foundling. He had been found in the forest along with a brown-striped piglet from a wild boar's brood. He showed a remarkable fondness for his companion in distress, which did not save her life, for she was served for supper with an apple in her mouth within a week. Adèle personally adopted the pink pig and gave him his name, fixing a sprig of the flowering broom called *plante genet* over the manger where she cradled him. Brémand had the new pig-sty built and installed his guest in it. Plantagenet objected to being confined there from the start, and deliberately went off his food. Each day he dwindled, and Adèle, who had given him her heart, was in despair. Finally Plantagenet won the concession that he would be allowed to idle in the courtyard with the poultry as long as he did not frighten them, and provided that he learned to open and shut the door of his sty. Adèle taught him to perfect this trick in a fortnight.

Apart from this particular skill, Plantagenet had one outstanding gift. Nature had endowed him with a capacity for extraordinary speed, considering he was a pig. He could run faster than a horse, especially when he had a presentiment of danger. Owing to a timid disposition Plantagenet often had a presentiment of danger. The freedom to roam the courtyard which he had won was gradually extended until he was making frequent expeditions to the forest to visit the boar Grondin and his family, whom he liked to think of as his country cousins. But he was always very careful on no account to come face to face with his *bête grise* Hurlaud the wolf, having heard that Hurlaud had vowed to give himself a treat by savouring Plantagenet's lean hams as the starter to a banquet. Plantagenet was very attached to his hams, which he considered to be the best-developed part of his anatomy. And every time he thought he glimpsed in the forest the grey thatch of Hurlaud thoughtfully observing him from under a covert or at an angle to a path, he doubled on his tracks and galloped back hell for leather.

Hurlaud had never been able to gain a single pace on him in the frequent handicap races which followed this manœuvre, and could only retaliate by bestowing on Plantagenet the would-be scornful nickname of The Flying Pig, which did not really rank very high as abuse and could even be taken as a compliment. None of this tension escaped the notice of Brousse the hen-magpie, who was always scouring the woods on the look-out for situations from which she could provoke a little aggro. And since the magpie's wit was sourer, she coined for Hurlaud the more spiteful nickname of The Slug.

Apart from his gift of superporcine speed, Plantagenet did not give the impression of being very smart. He was easily puzzled. Quite ordinary behaviour by others shocked and astonished him, and he spent sleepless nights coming to terms with it. He was always trying to understand domestic animals and humans, but his cloudy interpretations thrust him into situations which were generally incredible and sometimes disastrous. In one particular area, however, he muddled through with surprising success. It seemed to him that if Maister and Madame Brémand and their farm servants showed so much interest in him, and nourished him with such good cheer, they were doing it for some purpose which was probably connected with the constant prodding by the servant Edmond, who seemed abnormally curious about the depth of the layer beneath the skin, which Plantagenet regarded as his undercoat. Since he could not fully appreciate the motive, he was cautious about co-operating until he had puzzled it out. Consequently he ate very moderately, maintained an admirably slim figure, and to the keen regret of all the adults on the farm showed no signs of developing into the stout fellow they all longed for him to become. By devious, if not roundabout, reasoning, Plantagenet had stumbled on the surest means of staying alive and enjoying his freedom.

Since Plantagenet liked being liked by Adèle, and copied her behaviour in every way, he had adopted at an early age his great concern for cleanliness and order, which was considered an acquired taste for a pig. He plucked up grass and weeds in the courtyard, cleaned the stones from any grain that had fallen on them, constantly tossed the litter to make and re-make his bed, and he was always very good at closing all doors behind him. One day, when the cur Hargneu had gone out to the fields with the varlets, Plantagenet accidentally overturned the mastiff's kennel, and discovered underneath it a mass of bones, stale bread and every sort of rubbish. He hurriedly threw all this waste into the garbage pit, carefully cleaned up the ground around the kennel and, glowing with innocent pride at the neatness of the result, waited for the dog's return. He modestly explained what he had done, and ventured a mild reproach regarding the creature's notion of hygiene.

Hargneu went out of his mind. He jumped on Plantagenet and bit him wherever he could get his teeth to meet. Absolutely astonished by this unforeseen behaviour of the cur, Plantagenet uttered a series of squeals which were so frightful that in no time all the household were out in the courtyard with pitchforks and cudgels in the certain belief that the wolves had invaded the place. Before they could weigh up the situation, Hargneu snatched the opportunity to heave Plantagenet into the cess-pool which was near the scene of the contest, and the pig took an unexpected and entirely disagreeable bath. As the slime closed over his head Plantagenet was positive that he was at the point of death, and when he eventually surfaced in that fearsome pit the sheer awfulness of the surroundings did nothing to change his mind. He gave vent for the first time in his life to a super-squeal of such volume, such shrillness and such torturing length that it was entirely unendurable to any ear of normal construction.

With eyes closed in torment and teeth on edge with acid, Maister Brémand seized Plantagenet by the ears. This only had the effect of making him scream at a pitch of even greater insupportability. With farm hands tugging at his trotters and his tail Plantagenet was finally dragged from his unsought ablutions. Still wailing in terror, the Flying Pig seemed this time literally to fly to his sty, where he buried himself completely under the straw in his hitherto neatly-made bed. In a state of high dudgeon he stayed there for a long period of self-inflicted confinement, refusing visitors, consolation and food, which had the result of making him still thinner and frankly uglier. And, like all people and pigs who are excessively sorry for themselves, he thought long and deeply on The Mystery Of Life, Nobody Understands Me, and other related subjects. Only Adèle's constant, un-demanding visits brought him any healing. It was at this time that the supposedly sceptical heart of Plantagenet skipped a beat that set it dancing in an entirely different ballroom. As unrealistically as any other battle-shocked soldier being nursed by any other angel, he began to intertwine fantasies about their personalities which did not altogether disperse when he came out of his hallucinosis.

2
Before Saint Andrew's Fair

The principal lords of the forest, under the quiet guidance of the owl Uhlan the Wise, President of the Council of Animals, were the wolf Hurlaud of the Great Woods, the wild boar Grondin, and the bear Flandrin – though Flandrin did not frequent the innermost recesses, since on his four pads he was five times as bulky as a man and on his hind feet as broad and as tall as a horseman. Amiable adjutants of the great lords were the agile Fulgent, prince of the foxes, and the falcon Bafrin the Noble, who acted as a sort of Mercury of the gods but with dignity and without Mercury's mischief. Mischief and malevolence were the province of the hen-magpie Brousse, a trouble-maker without a shred of conscience, a born hellion who lacked the slightest appreciation of the law of the forest.

For the forest lived under law. Law is a form of order, as Aristotle said, and good law must necessarily mean good order. No one imposed it. Everyone except Brousse understood it and kept it with understanding.

There were no 'rights' but there was instinct, and inborn respect. A deer had no 'right' not to be attacked by a wolf but he took every precaution not to be. Indeed he put up a far more effective strategy of defence against extinction than

was available to the young trees he destroyed by eating their
bark and fraying his antlers against them. When death came,
from disease or predators, the survivors accepted the
diminution of the herd. They did not forget the dead, and
they did not exaggerate the importance of the living in the
gross forms of self-pity which display themselves as
mourning, resentment and vengeance. A wolf did not
slaughter for fun, but for need. He did not make war, nor
decree game protection laws, for political or sporting
reasons. The only creature who played politics was Brousse,
and she was considered vicious because she gambled for
personal gain – for disproportionate power – against the
delicate balance of nature which said that in the forest there
were neither rewards nor punishments, only consequences.
There were no rights, but there was Right.

The castle of Crespin also lived under law, but under a
different system. There was no Right, but there were plenty
of rights. In the world of man laws were supposed to have
been made so that the strong should not always have things
their own way, but the strong had given themselves a good
start by saying that all the land was theirs anyway, and they
had an army to prove it, and they could do what they liked
with anyone on their land. Since there was no accepted
Right, which would have saved a lot of argument, weaker
men had to establish by clever pleading that they had a
'right' not to be given wrong treatment by the strong.
Before they could claim a right the weak men had to become
stronger, strong enough to do wrong things like banding
together, petitioning the lord, or committing acts of terror-
ism when the law specifically said that they had no right to
form an association, beg for lower taxation, or punish the
lord when he attacked their daughters. Once they were
strong enough to do the wrong things the law was changed
to say that they had a right to do these things, which were no
longer wrong. But if the lord could catch them before they

were strong enough, he could beat them by strength of arms, which proved that they had no right to the rights they claimed.

When there was a war everyone's rights were abolished by an Emergency Law except for the soldiers, who could do what they liked under Martial Law. Naturally the soldiers liked war, because this was the only time they were supposed to think, as long as what they thought of was something that would harm civilians. Even when there was peace, the castle of Crespin kept up a war against the wild animals, who had no rights at all, except the deer, who were declared by the lord to be his anyway and he had an army to prove it. Because man was the only animal who chased and killed other animals for amusement or sport, and the deer were the most amusing animals to be chased and killed, the lord of Crespin gave the deer the right not to be killed in the breeding season, and only to be killed by a good sport who had the lord's special permission to do so.

In the household of the farm of La Tranchée there were few rights except that the farmer, Maister Brémand, admitted that the farm really belonged to the lord of Crespin, Messire de Frébois, and was worth what the lord charged him for it, and the lord agreed in his turn that Maister Brémand could tell his farm hands to do what he liked. There was also a sort of right, which nobody mentioned because it was not written down in any book, that Maister Brémand's wife, Dame Matilda, could tell Brémand and anyone else to do what she liked. As far as Maister Brémand and Dame Matilda were concerned with Adèle, and Adèle with them, there was hardly any question of rights at all. Some mention of parental responsibility and daughterly obedience might occasionally be made by Maister Brémand, who was an excitable man who worried too much and therefore lost his temper easily, but not for long at a time. There was more concern with love, which Adèle thought far more

real than rights and duties, and far more obvious, because
she felt she was flowing with it like a well spring. She
perceived that her parents were lavishing it quite copiously,
too.

This is a paradox, that humans can be not only the
cruellest creatures but also the most loving. It has something to do with the situation of Adam and Eve after the
Garden of Eden when the Lord declared, rather regretfully,
that these people would be as gods, knowing good and evil,
knowing it far more keenly than other creatures. So, while
man is the only animal who kills for fun or politics, he is
also the only animal who knows he is going to die, and that
his wife will some time die, and his daughter. This can make
people fearful or rebellious or sentimental. But it can also
make them transpire love, which is secreted by the understanding of death just as the implantation of a cub or a baby
secretes milk in a mother. Adèle was flowing with such a
flood of love that without ever thinking it was extraordinary she included in her affections the pig Plantagenet.
Maister Brémand did consider his daughter was going a bit
far, though he admitted to mixed feelings about Plantagenet,
partly as pet, partly as pork. What he did not realize (but
Adèle did) was that he had almost reached the intensity of
his daughter in his own affection for an English beagle named
Rupert. As for Dame Matilda, she called them both unnaturally mawkish, and daily lit a candle for her dead son.

Maister Brémand cheerfully whistled to Rupert the
beagle as he mounted his horse in late afternoon and rode
off to take pot-luck supper and any gossip that was going at
the house of his most prosperous neighbour among the outlying farms, Maister Pineau. With the dog at his side –
Rupert was not the type to run to heel – Brémand made a
wide circuit to reach his destination. The short cut through
a curving pocket of the forest did not appeal to him, though
it was a recognized path, important enough to connect with

the principal route to the market town. But even this main
road was a furtive, feeble track, dodging through brushwood
and thickets, twisting between disdainful oaks which it took
good care not to graze. It was never properly maintained, so
the undergrowth steadily advanced to take it over, the
young shoots nibbled at it little by little, and the huge trees
spreading unlopped overhead darkened it with their canopy.

Yet twice a year it stirred briefly into a feverish liveliness.
Just before the fairs in May and November the tough
wagoners from Beauchamp occupied it almost solidly all
the way to the market town, shouting and cudgelling as they
drove their enormous white oxen, yoked to the carts of
those of the neighbouring farmers who had hired them.
They took to the town wheat from Les Girolles, barley from
Le Busseau, kid-goats from Granzay and geese from Gript.
What with the shepherds and cattle drovers and the private
traffic, it was then an almost uninterrupted procession
lasting perhaps two days, sometimes three if it had been a
good year.

The expedition occupied people's minds for weeks in
advance. The inhabitants of the hamlets and isolated farms
would meet in the evening at the house of one or other of
them, and slowly get to know each other again over bacon
soup and a drop of reviver. In front of a hearth where elm
stumps were slowly burning away they would chat about
everything and nothing, not wanting to reveal too much of
their affairs too soon. Sometimes, with the help of new
wine, the tone of the conversation rose. When Brémand
arrived at Maister Pineau's the atmosphere, though still
guarded, was beginning to be social.

Every one was privately calculating his prospect of
coming into his money, of realizing his profit on the harvest
and on the livestock he had raised. The essential need was
to do good business at the coming fair, to sell well for Saint
Andrew. That decided the style in which they would spend

the winter. And of course, ancient tradition could not be betrayed – so everyone grumbled.

It had been a middling year, no more. Grain should just about make a profit but poultry might hardly show any return. The fields had never recovered from the Spring drought. So-and-so was making up husk to bring the fodder up in bulk. Landsakes, he was not the only one. Old Whatsisname was doing the same at Les Grévises.

The gossip rolled on in full spate. Soon it would be time to harness up for the great autumn fair. Then the truth would be known.

But first they would have had to accomplish the passage through The Forest.

A sudden silence fell on everyone around the tables. A man unnecessarily cleared his throat. Another set himself to cutting his nails conscientiously with his knife, in an air of great absorption. The Forest. The magic, taboo word had just been spoken. A sudden heaviness in the atmosphere seemed to dull everyone's spirits. No one seemed to want to break the silence, as if they could preserve its spell by avoiding mention of the . . . Thing. Couldn't that be put off until later? But the subject had to be tackled.

'The path seems to be in bad condition,' growled Maister Henriot. Rupert the beagle pricked up his ears at this. He understood Henriot better than the other strangers because Henriot hated him, partly because of his English ancestry, partly because of his English reserve – a tendency not to wag his tail so hypocritically as other dogs – but mostly because Rupert had been given to Brémand by their mutual lord, Messire de Frébois of the castle of Crespin, and Henriot had looked in vain for a parallel gift. 'It will do us no good to follow the track and then drown at Stags Crossing,' Henriot continued. 'The rain of the last days will have turned the crossing into marshland, you can be sure of that. We shall just get bogged down in last year's ruts. It would take a mort of time and labour to fill up that swamp with faggots.'

'It would be better to go through Malperthuis,' suggested a diffident bearded man whom Rupert recognized as Clément the sage-grower. 'There at least the ground is good. Of course it is a far longer way round. . . .'

'And when you get to town all those people from the plain will have sold at fancy prices,' snapped a woman's voice. It was the Widow Bigotte and she went on to rub in the bad news. 'There is no question of driving the flocks through Stags Crossing. It is crawling with wolves. Lucas and Jobert were there on Thursday. They went to cut back the undergrowth on the track. They saw some wolves there, and fearless wolves, by damn, or else with the cheek of the Devil. They were only two paces away under the covert, actually watching them while they were working. They had a good fright, I can tell you. Wolves, remember, it was wolves last year that took three of my lambs.'

The voice of the Widow Bigotte clattered on, making mountains out of modest hills of disaster, until the hour struck for her assassination of the sage-grower Clément.

'There are certain people who prefer the road through Malperthuis. I happen to understand them inside out. All *their* wealth is in the carts, guarded by men and dogs. *They* are not going to be the victims that the wolves make off with. *They* haven't any livestock to lose except their own miserable selves and you can bet they'll have guards enough to save their own skins. They talk about going by Malperthuis. What does it matter to them that the route is longer? Sacks will weigh the same when they arrive. But as far as we who raise livestock are concerned, each beast will lose a good two pounds weight a day in working himself to death in this way. The longer they take to get there the less we have to sell, and we all know what a sorry state they arrive in. I wonder His Eminence doesn't ordain that we

cross the Guirande at Souligné and start a pilgrimage to
the ford at Beauchamp.'

A low murmur which had been developing through the
last few sentences swelled to a disapproving uproar which
drowned the final words so that no one had opportunity to
consider whether they contained a good suggestion or not.
La Bigotte was well known as a greedy widow with an
extremely dry heart, which was not absolutely demon-
strable, and very desiccated legs, which were. Ill-disposed
gossip had it that even her husband had left this world not
unwillingly after fifty years of thin affection, hard words
and miserly treatment.

'Come on, come on,' Pineau the host interrupted to
jolly them up – and he had a good start, for there was no
doubt that he was the best off of all in his land holdings.
'We're not going to quarrel or whine at such a time as this.
I suggest we make up two convoys. One, the flocks and
herds, will go to town by way of Stags Crossing. The other,
with heavy cargo, will go by Malperthuis. We'll split up our
forces to escort them. I myself can put in a tidy few men.'
His tone was assured and his confidence was infectious.
'Wolves? It would be a pretty sight to have some of those
rapscallions show their grey wigs from out of a bush. They'd
get a very warm welcome.'

A general burst of laughter saluted the host's bravado.
Everyone got down to discussing the detailed organization
of the convoys.

3

The First Turn of the Screw

The dry, cold north wind of autumn which in Poitou they called La Bise had taken over from the rain and had succeeded in loosening the last leaves clinging to the dripping trees. They strewed the ground to make a slightly soggy carpet on which Grondin the wild boar trod with the greatest appreciation, for he particularly relished this season. The wind had not taken all the dampness out of the air. A whitish vapour rose from the ground of the glade which the boar had selected for his operations, giving off a sour smell of old grass and damp bark. The huge black bulk of Grondin could hardly be seen in the mist as he ferreted here and there, his snout under the leaves, searching for fresh acorns that had fallen overnight.

But a pair of sharp eyes had been keeping him under observation, and a grating voice sawed down through the murk into his ears:

'Ah! Squire Grondin! You're an early bird. Bird! He-he-he!' The imitation laughter rattled unconvincingly like the patter of a comedian who has lost all faith in audiences. 'What are you doing in this neck of the woods? You're three leagues off target. Has the crop failed at Les Combles, or has one of your heavies hogged it all?

A corner in acorns! Who's playing the market? Not *you*, Squire?'

Grondin the boar was a tough character, solitary, possibly sad, reputedly sinister. No one, not even Hurlaud the wolf and his pack, cared to pick a quarrel with him. They kept at a respectable distance from his formidable tusks. His three hundred pounds of leather-clad flesh made him practically invulnerable. He was not used to being called 'Squire' unless the speaker meant what he said, nor to being twitted about his foraging habits. Normally he would have reacted to such impertinence with a damaging toss of his snout. But he was not on his own territory, and he knew it. And he had an idea that his interlocutor was more agile than the creatures who usually crossed his path. He shot a baleful eye up to where the shrill voice had come from.

It was Brousse, the hen-magpie, who had spotted and followed him during a routine sweep from her nest in the high beech near Pied du Fût.

'Mischief-making gossip,' Grondin told himself. This shrew traded in nothing but gall and impudence. But because she was always poking and prying she knew most of what was going on in the world of the forest. She might serve a turn.

'No one knows better than you, good dame,' said Grondin forcing himself to be amiable, 'that there is no shortage of acorns at Les Combles. But at the moment I am on the look-out for a certain item of information.'

'I could be of use to you,' said Brousse with sudden interest. And with a twitch of her long tail she dropped three branch-heights.

'I am rather puzzled,' said Grondin, 'that as yet no one at the castle has raspberried into that comic hunting-horn and unleashed those idiot dogs on my heels. We all recognize the season. For ten years past, as soon as the coverts go bare, they have set themselves to making me pound the plain. This silence bodes no good, and I'm interested in finding out the reason.'

'Oh, *that!*' said the bird, simpering in a rather superior fashion. 'With respect, good Squire, these folks at the castle have more on their mind at the moment than making one hulk of boar sweat in his crackling.'

Grondin started with an imperceptible jump. This tree-arab, this egg-filcher was going a bit strong. His snout began to quiver with rage. But she was keeping herself a little too high for him to put it to use.

'Oh, and what goes on then?' asked Grondin in a tone he was trying to make detached.

'It's not a simple business. Soon it is the bean-feast of Saint Andrew in the town, and they are already preparing the wagon trains.'

'I don't see that that has anything to do with it.'

'That hardly surprises me,' said the magpie scornfully. 'Your lot at Les Combles are so busy filling their bellies that you can't keep up with the news.'

Grondin kept still, ready to leap, his eyes smoking.

'This is the season,' Brousse went on, 'when Hurlaud and his merry gang go a-mugging in the undergrowth, a-massacring in the glades and a-mopping up in the clearings. They even go down to the plain.'

'Schnozzle!' snorted Grondin. 'What has that to do with me?'

The magpie exploded into a frightening sound which on the other side of the ocean would have been instantly identified as rattlesnakes on the rampage. The bird was, in fact, laughing – or doing the best she could. 'What has that to do with you?' she cackled. 'It would have something to do with you if Messire de Frébois, the darkly handsome warlike lord of Crespin, decided to take up arms against a sea of Hurlauds NOT EXCLUDING HIS PALS and led an army to run you out of the country as the best they could do – and I could think of much worse they could do, dear Squire. It would have something to do with you if you lost thirty pounds on the run you'd need to take to get away from them.' The magpie choked with helpless laughter and shook in apparent pain for some seconds before recovering sufficiently to add: 'Not, I suppose, that you'd even notice losing thirty pounds.'

'And so?' said Grondin, menacingly quiet. His tone penetrated the galloping delirium which seemed on the point of overcoming the magpie, and with a flurry of black-and-white she flew up two hands higher to a safer altitude.

'And so,' said Brousse with her eyes very sharply focussed on the boar to register the effect of her words, even if she chose to clothe them in fortune-teller's tinsel. 'And so it could be that, a roadway off, what you don't expect will happen in a trey. In three somethings: three weeks, three days, three hours, three MINUTES,' Brousse hummed and hissed with menace, 'a dark man, quick to anger, not to be provoked with importunity, will, as the result of a misfortune through caprice, and inflamed with drunkenness and debauchery, bring disappointment and vexation, possibly leading to sickness and death, certainly causing a removal by land, to a Person of portly proportions, advised in the nick of time by a sincere Friend of fair complexion, who in spite of the great danger she risks for her imprudence, is by no means a selfish and deceitful fraud, but will deliver unexpected good news that may avert the disappointment and vexation, sickness and death, removal and ruination, at a further clandestine encounter, if the Person sincerely wants a successful outcome attained by the virtuous discretion of the candid Friend with the fair complexion.'

'FAIR!' said Grondin, gazing at the magpie. 'Which half? How do you pick up all this private-dick prittle-prattle? You can claim about as much camouflage as a black-and-white minstrel.' But Grondin's heavy raillery could not mask how perturbed he was.

Brousse shifted her eye and admired herself from head to foot. She preened her feathers and remarked to the boar with insufferable condescension: 'I have a couple of gadgets which enable me to ride high and fast and see a great deal of the world. You should invest in a pair of flappers yourself. Though you'd have to fit yourself out with a monster set even to hoist your carcase as high as this branch, where I can see you're dying to call on me.'

Mad with frustration, Grondin charged the tree in the vague hope that he might knock Brousse off her perch. The oak shook under the shock but the bird had already taken avoiding action. She rose with a flutter of wings and a final jeer: 'Keep your strength for running, Grondin. You may be doing the jogger's jig quite soon. But have no fear, Brousse is near, to bring you all the latest in your liquidation news. Don't call me, I'll call you. Fanfare, close-up, and out.'

All that Grondin got out of the encounter was a pain in his snout and a succession of uncomfortable thoughts. 'If ever one day,' he promised himself, 'that witch of doom falls into my hands, all that will be left will be just enough feathers to clothe a cricket.

'But, another thought! Suppose the wretched creature was speaking the truth!'

4
Passing the Buck

The pale day heaved itself up and laboriously paced over the autumn forest. The morning mist slowly lifted to leave only a thin white coverlet of velvet on the leafy ground, broken by black outcrops of dead wood.

Hurlaud stretched his limbs blissfully on the threshold of his lair in the heart of a dense thicket. Inside, a playful yapping and growling indicated that his youngest cubs were half-heartedly resisting the licking and cleaning which their mother Dame Pernale was assiduously applying.

The Hurlaud family, having dined the night before on one of the Widow Bigotte's sheep which had dared to put a foot in the undergrowth, was making its morning toilet. Slatted over the earth, the bones nibbled white, the scraps from the feast testified that they had enjoyed a banquet of royal proportions.

Tiny muscles moved in Hurlaud's face. His fine ear and sensitive nose informed him that Grondin was somewhere in the offing. He had little desire to tangle with the boar at any time, and even less now that hunger no longer nipped his stomach and he had provided for his family's needs for some time. He therefore chose to affect a haughty indifference, feigning complete unconcern about Grondin while keeping a wary look-out for the unpredictable reactions of this 'sack of leather', as he privately referred to the black boar.

Ever since his encounter with Brousse Grondin had not been able to digest his anger, still less his disquiet. Muttering to himself, he picked his way with short steps along the path. He was very well aware of the presence of the wolf, and realized he was passing close to his den. He had even glimpsed him, but he gave no sign of it.

'You're looking very well, Monseigneur,' Hurlaud observed when Grondin came up with him. 'Yes, indeed,' said the boar with a show of surprise at having seen him and boredom at having to engage in a conversation. 'Well, what's this? You seem to have had a very fine junketing.' He indicated with his snout the grisly remains which strewed the ground.

'Yes, to be sure. I had to deal vigorously with a marauder. Some scoundrel came to my home with I don't know what wicked intentions. I had to take strong action to defend myself. Believe me, this brute would have well and truly savaged me.'

The wolf's cynicism was too much for Grondin. He spoke more familiarly. 'Unprovoked aggression? Eh, now, do you want me to believe that, old man? Since when have your sort had to defend themselves against the belligerence of sheep? This is a new development. Are you into disarmament? Have you lost your cutlery?'

Hurlaud detonated into a great burst of laughter which revealed two dazzling rows of teeth as sharp as steel.

'You re-assure me,' commented Grondin. 'But I have something to tell you which will make you laugh on the other side of your face.'

'Has something happened to you, Monseigneur? You seem all out of sorts,' said the wolf, suddenly uneasy and inwardly poised to make a defensive leap.

'I have just been picking a bone with that two-faced

magpie, Brousse. That broody witch has the insolence of the Devil. But I have to admit she scavenges wide for her mischief. She has plenty of nerve. She'll squeeze herself into the thatch of the village houses and even has a hide-out in the chimney at the castle. She listens in on everyone and gets to know what's in the wind.'

'Such as?' said Hurlaud intently.

'Oh, not much at the moment,' said Grondin in an off-hand tone. 'Something might happen in the forest before the Feast of Saint Andrew.' Grondin stopped for a moment to snort, and then went on in an even more detached manner: 'It occurs to me that there may be some excitement in the forest and that you and yours will feel the need for fresh air if your legs can carry you far enough and fast enough.'

Hurlaud had lost some of his easy bearing. He was far from taking the matter as lightly as Grondin was indicating. He grimaced frightfully, sat down, and stayed a moment in silence. Grondin affected to be not at all alarmed. He remained standing, apparently very calm, and looked at Hurlaud with an air of sympathy and concern.

The wolf noticed it. This hideous bladder of fat was not going to get away with it like that. 'I can see,' he said, 'that I and my family may have to take certain necessary measures with some urgency. The respectful friendship I bear for you leads me also to think of *you*. If I and mine must run, we shall do it, Monseigneur. Be sure of that. Nature has provided us with the means for such an exit and we can do it very fast. There is no doubt that we shall be able to extricate ourselves from this bad business since you have had the extreme goodness to warn me of it. That said, Monseigneur, let me express to you not only all my gratitude but also all the fears which affect me on your account. You are of an age that commands my respect, indeed you are a veteran. But I have a painful suspicion that your legs are not going to carry you very far at the pace which those skinheads are likely to impose on us. If by good chance you do happen to reach the Guirande it will have taken a lot out of your fine condition. It grieves me to think that this admirable embonpoint, these gracious curves on which it delights me to compliment you in your portly presence, must suffer somewhat from your forced retreat; indeed that your compulsory slimming may go as far as a *reductio ad absurdum*.'

The tone was polite and considerate, giving Grondin no justification for being offended by it. The situation was in any case very embarrassing to him. Hurlaud's shrewd cut had severed his points. He could only clutch at his gaskins and forget about saving his face.

Grondin sullenly tossed his head. 'If what we hear is verified we all ought to fly,' he admitted, 'and the sooner the better. We must seize any opportunity. However, Messire, in this affair you carry a very heavy responsibility.'

Hurlaud opened his jaws to protest but Grondin did not give him time. 'Come off it!' he thundered in a crescendo of scandalized indignation. 'For three years past your packs have ravaged the woods and the plains. No one ventures in these parts without armed horsemen. Every convoy crossing the woods from Sansais to Maire has to have a heavy escort. If a flock wanders, your people immediately attack it. If a sheep grazes two paces away from its fellows, you pounce on it. You have gone out of your way to try the patience of the people around. You remember the carnage which your brothers perpetrated at Maister Lhuillier's just before last Christmas? Nothing that grunts, clucks or cackles survived. Add to that the abominable tricks you yourself have played on my cousin Plantagenet. Admit that we are all going to suffer for the atrocities which you and yours have committed.'

'Calm yourself, calm yourself, Monseigneur. Nothing is perfect and everyone has his weaknesses. Is it my fault that

I cannot live on acorns? Have you never heard the groans of
our starving children? It's enough to make one give up the
ghost. I live in the forest and do no harm at all. But if they
harm me I make myself felt. That seems quite fair to me.
This Lhuillier is notorious as avaricious and depraved, a
thoroughly bad master. Even his mastiff Fussault says so.
Do you think I'm inventing it? As for that sheep of yester-
day or the day before, well, I may have exaggerated its
aggression. But the farm can afford it and the Widow
Bigotte is a hag and a witch. Everyone knows that, too.
Indeed, it has come to my ears that in liberating that
wretched ewe I have prompted many a worthy cheek to
crease in an approving chuckle around the hearths in the
village. For the sake of my starving children what was I
supposed to do? Go for the woman herself? On her own
account she wouldn't yield more than ten pounds of very
tough meat. So I took a sheep. Well, a lamb or two as well,
they would have been miserable without their mother.
Pooh, it's a nothing.

'As for your cousin the pig: on that point, Monseigneur,
I beg you to do me justice. This Plantagenet is the stupidest
animal I know. I hadn't the slightest intention of eating him,
only of frightening him. What harm is there in that?'

Having launched on the stream of eloquent advocacy,
Hurlaud kept on his course. 'I venture to say that I ought
not to be singled out as the only creature who has provoked
what now threatens us,' he observed with dark shades of
innuendo. His voice dropped into a confidential tone. 'It
appears that only last September, near Château Crespin, on
Michaelmas Night, a number of credible witnesses saw,
thanks to the light of the moon – hold tight, Monseigneur –
five or six black hulks systematically turning over a field of
beets. It seems that a great deal of damage was done.
Malicious informers immediately reported the matter to the
castle. It could be that Messire de Frébois was transported

to a great pitch of anger at this exploit, and he may have decided to call up a specially organized force to deal with these despoilers.' In a still more muffled voice, and with an eye feigning deep sympathy Hurlaud concluded: 'Rest assured that I don't believe a word of this tale, but anyone credulous enough to accept it may feel justified in undertaking extraordinary measures.'

Grondin suddenly found himself choking, and began noisily clearing his throat amid signs of the greatest embarrassment. That field of beets certainly stood out among his memories. But how had this conniver Hurlaud got wind of it? The boar realized that, far from triumphing as a prosecuting attorney, he had suddenly been lumbered with a desperate defence, and he needed an urgent adjournment for consultation with his client. Since he did not wish to be seen talking to himself in public he pleaded a violent attack of indigestion and he made his hurried adieux. 'God keep you, Hurlaud, you and yours.'

'And you, too, Monseigneur,' said the wolf more obsequiously than ever, and as he bowed he tucked his muzzle behind his fore right pastern, the better to laugh in his sleeve.

5
Family Circles

Grondin was not what educators call a bright character, but neither was he stupid. He was the salt of the earth in the days before that phrase was snatched by the élite to describe lesser fry who would die to defend them. Grondin would die in defence of his territory and his family – though, being a boar, he was no great family man – but he would not die thoughtlessly nor if he could work out the slightest chance of preserving what he was attached to and saving his life at the same time. Because he was not bright he was not over-sensitive. Because he was not stupid he knew that the only important event of the day, and that uncorroborated as yet, was the hint of a foray into the forest by the mandrakes and the consequent need to plan to survive. Because he was the salt of the earth his outlook was salty and mature. The fact that Hurlaud had played against his slower wit to tie him in knots was worth remembering but not resenting. Grondin could accept that. He accepted many reverses and dis-comfitures – possibly more than really existed, for his philosophy always chose the more pessimistic interpretation if there was a choice. The future of Plantagenet was an instance. As Grondin made his slow way towards his home ground at Les Combles he caught a faint whiff of Plantagenet, and immediately sketched a scenario putting the worst possible construction on the goodwill of Maister Brémand.

The farmer who at that moment was feeding and sheltering Grondin's white cousin had thus far shown apparent kindness but, Grondin had no doubt, the wretch had a sordid and sinister purpose at heart.

The farm itself, the domaine of La Tranchée, was at that time plainly visible from the skirts of the forest, all gold in the clear, flat autumn sunlight. But Grondin was not the character to enjoy any man-made thing of beauty even if the panorama was recommended as worth a detour. In any case, he accepted that he was too short-sighted in his peepers. He did not spare the farm a glance. However he smelt it judicially, like a wine-taster who has been mauled in a family quarrel at breakfast but is trying to be fair to the rest of the world. He spat and passed on.

Plantagenet, who had been rescued from sulking in his sty by the trick of a trip in his heart, was now basking in the full realization that he loved everybody because he was bound to Adèle. This is the most rewarding aspect of the enchantment of young love, before the twin roes of autocracy and jealousy soil the lilies they feed on. Plantagenet wanted to demonstrate the loving kindness he felt for all creatures here below, and the recipients of his visible friendship necessarily had to include a dog. Correctly reasoning that the time was hardly ripe for Hargneu to fall into his embrace, Plantagenet was seized with the desire to make a generous present to a dog called Pommard living at the farm of Les Voiries. Among the pig's daily rambles of exploration he had been in the habit, some time ago, of including a trip to the far forest of Chizé by way of the woods around Les Fosses. During these expeditions he had made the acquaintance of the dog Pommard at his farm midway between home and the clearing of Paitout. After a few well-bred civilities Pommard had very kindly invited Plantagenet to share his meal at the farm. This friendly action had so impressed the pig that he now decided to collect all the bones, bread and different

eatables that he could find at La Tranchée to make a gift of
them to his newly-remembered companion.

Since there would be some difficulty in carrying his gifts,
and he was good at opening and shutting doors, he decided
to borrow the *cabas*, the long flat basket, which Dame
Matilda had hung up conveniently to hand – or in
Plantagenet's case to snout – in the corridor. A further
thought reminded him that bread and bones might be un-
hygienic, and it seemed better to help himself from Dame
Matilda's larder. He blithely filled the basket with sausages,
cheeses and delicate pâtés carefully stacked there for
Christmas, choosing with discernment the dishes which
seemed to him most appropriate for the palate of his fine
friend. Occasionally he was in honest doubt, asking himself
if this crusty pie, for instance, would have the luck to please
Pommard, and could only make up his mind after taking a
small sample himself. He completed his selection, and
turned to go with the creaking basket. And face to face in
the corridor he met Maister Brémand, who had returned
unexpectedly.

Brémand – it was an admitted failing of his – was endowed
with a lively temper which flared as soon as there was a hint
of any one tampering with his possessions. He understood
what Plantagenet had done, if not where he was going.
There followed a proprietorial duffing-up, enlivened by
colourful shrieks from Plantagenet who was protesting in
his own language the purity of his intentions. The uproar was intensified by high howls of laughter from the
abominable Hargneu, who was enjoying the whole episode
immensely. Extricating himself from the bastonnade with
desperate agility, Plantagenet streaked towards his sty and
dived deep under the straw.

After having been unjustly beaten for trying to do a good
deed, there seemed clear justification for another spell of
sombre reflections on The Mystery of Life. But the bliss of

appreciating Adèle still suffused him and, although there were moments of black rebellion and profound philosophy, cheerfulness kept breaking in. He resolved that there was no point in negatively asking the sty from under two feet of straw Why Was I Born? The sty made no response at all. It would be far better to bring matters into the open, get out into the world, and Do Something About It.

Plantagenet opened his mouth to look at the weather and test the time of day. With his permanent undercoat he never felt the draught, or a change of temperature, until long after he should have done something about it, and his eye did not have the range of the sailors who looked on tempests at La Rochelle. He tasted a fair day, noticeably shortening after the autumn equinox, scattered sunlight, zephyr increasing to breeze Force One, time nearer Nones than Vespers. The signs favoured a visit to his cousin Grondin.

Grondin was away but he had left his wife and family to mind the home, and Plantagenet stood chatting. Dame Albaine was taking life easy in her forest glade, lounging in a shallow dug-out lined with dry moss. A number of other sow matrons were within gossiping distance. Their youngsters were becoming restless with the turn of the afternoon and were beginning some mild mischief. Pielet, the liveliest of the litter of Albaine and Grondin, at the age of six months still wearing his juvenile colours of fawn-and-brown long stripes as if he had carelessly lain on a hot grill to try it for size, was actively eroding his mother's good temper.

More than once she interrupted her conversation with Plantagenet to give a bark that warned Pielet to mind his manners. Plantagenet always envied Albaine for this bark, which he had tried to practise when day-dreaming plots against the bullying mastiff, Hargneu. But the fact that he could not do it was not really one of the sad signs that showed he was different. None of the wild boars, not even

Grondin, could manage that bark. Only the sows could
do it.

'Do sit down,' said Dame Albaine, and Plantagenet
stretched sociably in the long hollow of Grondin's dry-grass
divan. It seemed that the bed had not been made for days,
or perhaps it was just that the children had been boisterous.
Often Grondin did not come home at nights, not because
he was a bad father but because for seven or eight months
of the year all wild boars are loners. They have a pretty
solitary disposition, just foraging and thinking, not mixing
much even with other boars. ('I wouldn't mind so much if
he even went to the *Club*,' Dame Albaine confided to
Plantagenet.) They acknowledge their responsibility for
social security and keep in touch with the herd, but only
re-join the community on a full-time basis for the long and
sometimes obstreperous festival of the mating season,
which starts in late autumn. 'I have to set my cap at him all
over again,' lamented Dame Albaine. 'Why don't we wild
boars kick into this Till-Death-Us-Do-Part caper that the
wolves have had for ages? Pernale and Hurlaud have been
together all their lives. And look what a smoothie Hurlaud
is. If he *wanted* to. . . .'

Suddenly Plantagenet plunged nervously. Dame Albaine
knew what was going on, and barked at young Pielet.
'Wait till your father gets home,' she threatened. 'I'm
waiting,' he retorted.

'These kids will be the death of me,' she howled to the
entire glade of sows, as if she were announcing her extinction
by suttee: but the sows took no notice. Pielet had discovered
Plantagenet's tail and was exploring it with fascination. It
was curly, and the only pig-tails Pielet knew hung straight
and straggly as tarred rope. How did that tail manage to keep
a perfect strong circle, as round as the moon? Was there a
spring inside, like a spruce shoot? You could put your snout
right through that ring, and it was warm. Rather comforting

in a daring sort of way, a bondage you knew you could break – or did you know? . . . better try. After a reconnaissance of the tail as nose-band Pielet began deep research on the tip as snaffle. He used his teeth. The lower tusks were razor-sharp through grinding on the upper canines. Plantagenet leapt into the air. Without the speed and strength of the pig's rocketing take-off Pielet could never have accomplished the polished surgery which was now revealed. The end of Plantagenet's tail was neatly circumcised and skinned. Dame Albaine, who had struggled up in alarm at Plantagenet's meteoric rise, literally fell on her son in rage at his rudeness to a guest. But in mercy she did not utilize her full carcase. One hundred pounds of best gammon entirely obliterated Pielet. Not a squeal emerged.

The bleeding, but kindly, Plantagenet decided to depart at once, as the only way to give his invisible nephew a chance of survival. 'Grondin is in the far glade?' he confirmed from Albaine.

'Down through the tree tunnel,' she said. 'Along Badgers' Walk, and the first clearing after Avenue Hurlaud. You can't miss him.' And she heaved herself off Pielet, who lay still, as flat as a rug, waiting to be beaten.

Plantagenet would have put in a good word for his nephew but his mind had been distracted by the last name in Albaine's directions. Suddenly he did not want to go any farther. But Albaine was looking at him with warm concern, and even one eye in the rug of Pielet was open and observing him. Plantagenet was embarrassed at appearing to have turned against their husband and father. As an excuse, he went off the road into an arbour of convolvulus as if he wanted to excuse himself, and he found that it was no excuse at all but the real thing. He took the opportunity to have a little think.

'Avenue Hurlaud!' he told himself. 'What senseless

glorification of a hun, a vandal, what a monument to a
public enemy! The next thing, they'll be calling the forest
ride Death Row. Steady, old boy, it's just nonsense really.
Don't let it frighten you. It's only a name. But names should
be pleasant, like the sweet sound that breathes upon a bank
of violets. When I am king I shall re-name it Avenue Adèle.
No, first I shall be a prince, and my fairy godmother will
transform Adèle into the beautiful sow she always was
before the witch's curse, and we shall be . . . oh, it's too
deliriously exciting to. . . . But have I the courage? Can I
ever be a fit mate for Adèle? I haven't even the courage to go
into the brushwood, let alone the tree tunnel and A . . .
A . . . All that lies beyond, Ave . . . Ave. . . . Ora pro nobis.'

Plantagenet took the track through the undergrowth at a
very fast rate. He pretended to himself that he was only
practising a speed-burst, as demonstrated by the squires in
the running races organized to warm up the dull start of a
tournament while the lord was still at lunch. And when he
came through to the clearing he twisted his snout into a
grin to the right and a snort to the left as he breasted an
imaginary tape amid the applause of an imaginary grand-
stand while, fluttering against the blue of an even more
mistily fantastic pavilion, a white rose for a white pig fell
from the fingers of a swooning Adèle. In spite of the wild
(and imaginary) acclamation, however, there was a bristling
of his hairs and an intensity in his pink eyes that could have
been dubbed the Hurlaud syndrome.

Grondin was standing stock still in the silted remnant of a
small pool from which all the water seemed to have been
drained. His huge bulk was as cased in mud as if he had been
modelled in clay. Some patches were lighter than the rest,
where the heat of his hide had dried them.

'Are you morose?' asked Plantagenet.

'Not today, I'm Grondin. Come on in,' said Grondin.
The mud is fine.'

'There's none left,' said Plantagenet.

'Plenty more where that came from. There's a hole over there. All you have to do is keep your eyes open.'

'Sometimes I do better with them shut,' said Plantagenet. 'Are you having a wallow?'

'Do I look as if I'm having a wallow?'

'No.'

'Then why ask? "Wallow: to roll about in mud, sand, water; to take swinish delight in sensuality." I *have* been having a wallow. I *have* been rolling in swinish delight. I am not now wallowing. As you observed, I have used it all up.'

'As *you* observed, there's plenty more where that came from. All you have to do is keep your eyes open.'

Plantagenet considered that his cousin Grondin was in a good enough mood to absorb this daring repartee. The next moment, he feared he was mistaken. With incredible speed there was a revolution in the boar's neck and a bright white tusk whistled up the side of Plantagenet's loin. But the pig was untouched. Like a lord chief justice fixing a man before sentence, Grondin allowed one eye to penetrate Plantagenet's heart and see if it was trembling. 'H'm,' he commented with approval. 'You're getting steadier.' He favoured Plantagenet with his other eye as well. 'You've come to see me about something?'

'Yes, cousin Grondin.'

'Sit down and we'll have a pow-wow.'

Even the thought of sitting down gave Plantagenet an excruciating pain in his raw, skinned tail. 'Not sit, if you don't mind,' he said, generously wiping the name of Pielet from his tongue. 'Been sitting all day. Could do with a stretch. Will take the pow-wow.'

'Do you mind if we dine first? We can pow politely as we munch and have the real wow while we take an after-dinner stroll.'

'Just as you like,' said Plantagenet cautiously. 'But I shall have to be back at La Tranchée before the drawbridge goes up.' He had no wish at all to eat at that moment. He had enough trouble in riding the displeasure of Maister Brémand at the large amount of his daily ration which he left untouched.

'Now what do you fancy?' asked Grondin. 'Roots, fruits or nuts?'

'I'll take pot luck. I'm not particularly hungry.'

'What did you have for breakfast?'

'Oh, just my mash.'

'Your mash? What's that?'

'Sixty-five per cent barley meal, twenty-five per cent wheat middlings, ten per cent white-fish meal.'

'You're joking!'

'I wish I were,' said Plantagenet fervently.

'Well, dip where you wish. I've always been a good trencherman myself.' Grondin proved his claim immediately by turning over an upper layer of soil with his snout as neatly as the coulter of a new-model plough, snipping constantly with his front teeth which chattered like barbers' scissors, and heaving with the sabres of his tusks to cut out and lift root vegetation. Workmanlike in his eating without being offensively greedy, Grondin had little time for the polite pow he had promised, except to indicate promising dessert prospects to Plantagenet. 'Very good seam of bracken laid down here,' he grunted. 'I calculate it at forty-five tons an acre at a depth within reach of your average boar.' Expertly he laid back the earth, swiftly trenched and mined, exposing the white starchy rootstock of bracken, which he chewed with thoughtful appreciation.

'Now,' he said to Plantagenet when they both declared themselves satisfied. 'I suppose you've come to ask about your father?'

'How did you know that?' gasped Plantagenet.

'Everybody asks about his father sooner or later.'

'It's just that I'm so different.'

'Different from whom? Your father?'

'I suppose so. I don't know. From you, anyway.'

'Does it matter?'

'I'm not so strong as you. Not so hardy. Not so independent.'

'Does that matter?'

'It matters to me.'

'What's the point of being strong, hardy, independent – and bloody bad-tempered at times, too, I may add – when you live on a farm with a pretty girl making a silk purse out of your ear and her father stuffing you with – did you *really* say ten per cent white-fish meal?'

'I should never have accepted the farm if I hadn't been . . .' Plantagenet hesitated.

'Queer? Handicapped? Illegitimate?' said Grondin remorselessly.

'Different,' said Plantagenet stolidly. 'White. Delicate. Feeble.'

'Unwanted,' said Grondin, piling on the agony.

'Well, I *wasn't* wanted, was I? Anyone can see that. I must have come from bad stock. My mother didn't want me. What about my father?'

'Have you ever thought that you *were* wanted?' asked Grondin. 'That you *are* wanted? Even admired? White, delicate, feeble – though with a remarkable turn of speed. I saw you coming into that clearing, you know, as if you were being chased by the clappers of hell.' Plantagenet cheered up considerably at that reference until he realized that Grondin was probably speaking the literal truth. 'White, delicate, feeble – you'd be hard pushed to hold your own as a boar out here, harder pushed to claim a mate in the shenanigans over the next few months. You're doing all right in La

Tranchée. You're in an environment that suits you. You've got freedom, you've got ten per cent fish meal, you've got every opportunity to visit your relations. . . .'

'Relations!' said Plantagenet bitterly.

'What do you mean?'

'Well, *are* they my relations? Are you?'

'We're animals, aren't we?' asked Grondin cruelly. '*Animalis sum; animalis nil a me alienum puto*. No part of the animal world is out of my empathy. What more do you want?'

'Relations,' said Plantagenet, miserably.

'All right,' said Grondin in a far less aggressive tone. 'You want to know about your father. Who doesn't? Now I *know*, but I can't prove it, exactly who your father was. He was a rakehelly bounder called Tuhart who was blood brother to my own father – so you're my cousin all right, cousin Plantagenet – and he was killed in a boar hunt when he was covering the retreat of your mother before you were born. I know that, but I can't prove it, and neither can anybody else about his begetter. But if it's a wise pig who knows his own father, it doesn't take much cunning, owing to the munificence of nature, to know one's own brothers and sisters. Because, unlike our fellow artiodactyls the large red deer, we are not born one at a time, not single spies but in battalions, springing out in showers as a joyful sign that father hit the jackpot. There were born with you Niort, Claire, Achouart, Quetton, Rance, Pochin and sweet Hortense, who was unfortunately and accidentally overlaid and smothered by your mother soon after birth. I know, because I was an inquisitive young rip and I was there: at the birth and at the smothering. All the piglets wore the usual striping except you and you were white, old sport, and I never stopped wondering for a week. But if you *hadn't* been wanted, don't you think it would have been dead easy to overlay and smother *you* instead of or in addition to sweet

Hortense? Why, your mother kept a special nipple for you, trespassers being persecuted. Be your age. Don't freak out for martyrdom.

'As for your poor dead father, you wouldn't have got much sympathy from him even if he had lived, so you're not missing much. It just doesn't happen with our lot. We are not a demonstrative family, particularly the dear old dads. Look at all us boars mooching about on our own. We just ain't sociable, to our sons or anyone else, certainly not to our fathers. You're different? You're lucky! It's my nature. I think a boar first quarrels with his father about four months before he is born. That's when he insists on setting up a separate establishment. There's no going back after that. The more complete the separation, sometimes the better for both.'

Grondin paused.

'Do you feel any better after enduring that unaccustomed public speaking?'

'Much better, cousin Grondin.'

'I don't feel bad myself.'

The two stood side by side, nose to tail, for a formal moment. Grondin nobly said nothing about Plantagenet's raw extremity. They turned to face each other and survey their surroundings.

There was a profound calm throughout the forest as if all natural enmity had been suspended for a period of bliss. The sunlight filtered through the foliage without bluster or annoyance. A pale yellow beech leaf, falling a full month before it was necessary, floated languorously down like a capricious fairy reserving her choice of landing-field until the last moment. There was a whirr of a heavy bird's wings above, and a shower of early beech nuts pattered to the ground.

'At times like this,' Grondin observed, 'I feel God is being very generous: a balmy evening; the sheer unnecessary delightful extravagance of the line of that leaf in flight; the smiling scattering of beech nuts as a promise of so many more to come.'

'Do you praise God in the beech?' asked Plantagenet.

'We happen to be standing under a beech tree. If we saunter along, we shall be under another. There may be a god in the beech or God may be in the beech. In either case I praise him. If we cross over the ride, we shall find a number of oaks. I'm never sure whether the acorn or the beech nut is God's greatest gift to swine. Possibly acorns for bulk satisfaction, beech nuts for delicacy. You may imagine a god in every oak tree as well as in every beech, in which case you should include every turnip, beetroot, rhizome of bracken, rootstock of couch grass, not to speak of the unsurpassable truffle.

'But add to that the fact that we are actively enjoying an autumn evening and a light spicing of philosophical conversation. In a lust for separatism do you perceive, construct, invent, and therefore praise a god of light philosophical conversation on an autumn evening? I find it more economical of thought – that is, sheer better design – to praise God: period. In that way we can accommodate the humans, and eliminate the need to create a god of roast pork.'

'Roast pork?' echoed Plantagenet.

'Yes. Humans happen to like it. It's hard on us but I can't convince myself that it's therefore immoral. We may consider roast pork a depraved taste, but is it more repulsive than Hurlaud's raw mutton? We may be creatures of high principle, but when it comes to dietary principles we keep remarkably quiet to the wolves. I fancy a snail myself, filthy carnivore that I must be. But is there revealed virtue in vegetarianism? How do I know that as I seize the succulent truffle under ground it does not scream like a mandrake to those who have ears to hear?

'No. We have no right to reserve God for swine and deprive man of grace in roast pork. Anyway, one universal god simplifies my religious principles. Praise God.'

'Praise God,' said Plantagenet. 'Praise God, all creatures here below.'

6

A Massacre Has Been Arranged

The castle of Crespin throbbed in a ferment of activity that had been steadily mounting for a week. Varlets bustled about, preparing stores of equipment and food. Ostlers were burnishing saddles, polishing harness, and currying horses which had lately been allocated double rations of oats every day. The old-timers among the men-at-arms applied themselves with ostentatious calm to checking boar-spears, bows and crossbows, then drilled with loud shouts in the courtyard to show the recruits just how military movements should be made. The servants and even the ladies of the castle busied themselves around the ovens and in the linen-room where the battle-hose and hunting-doublets were stored.

Away from the tumult, in the quiet of the great hall, earnest discussions went on between Messire de Frébois, Messire des Golletières and Messire des Chaussées, respectively the lords of the fiefs of Maire, Souligné and Frontenay. The reason for all this unaccustomed activity was the organization of a battue intended to rid the neighbouring forest once and for all of its undesirable inhabitants. Everything was planned in detail: the day, the place, the time, the disposition of the men and their reinforcements.

In preparation for this equerries in full dress had been despatched summoning to the castle of Crespin, the domaine of Messire de Frébois, all serfs, villeins, bondmen, tenants, stewards and every other able-bodied male resident in the fiefs concerned. Since it was intended that the operation should last at least two days, the lords had called on the burghers of the free towns to contribute to the personnel and maintenance of their force. Everyone responded to the summons, very excited to be bidden to such a junket. At the appointed hour they were all assembled on the polished benches of the great hall, listening in deep silence to the call to arms which their lord was addressing to them.

'Valiant and virtuous subjects of our fiefs,' Messire de Frébois began, 'our venerable neighbours Messire des Golletières and Messire des Chaussées, whom you see here, have after deliberation with me and Maître Lescure, seneschal of the town, whom you also see on my right, decided to give lasting protection to all our people, their land and their possessions.

'In the course of the past years many among you have had to deplore the ravages of the wild beasts which haunt our woods and at times prowl boldly under our walls. It has now become a matter of the utmost urgency to rid our lands for ever of the noxious animals which live and breed in the forest and put us in so much fear.'

A roar of acclamation greeted this announcement. Messire de Frébois savoured the approval for some time and then continued:

'We have therefore decided to impose a final solution of our problems before the festivities of Saint Andrew begin. It is insupportable that you should not be able to drive your flocks and produce to the town without being exposed to the incidents which over the past year have caused serious loss and provoked general indignation.

'Here, then, is the plan which our neighbours, our friends, and I myself have prepared:

'The operation will start on Thursday the fourth of November at seven ack-emma. All conscripted personnel will report to their appropriate castle by five ack-emma in order to have taken up the set positions in tight formation by seven ack-emma. The exercise will last two days and no leave of absence on any grounds will be granted during that period. The upkeep and subsistence of men and equipment is assured. The farms will be garrisoned only by non-combatant women and aged men, but an emergency flying column will be maintained in Castle Crespin to go to the aid of any location under threat of attack. Every able-bodied man, cropper, tenant and farmer will put himself at the disposal of the lord of his fief. In my sector you, Brémand, Henriot, Pineau, Jobert and Clément will be under my command.

'In detail, the operation will be conducted in this manner:

'Messire des Golletières will be responsible for the southern section of the forest between Vallans and Donkey Bottom. Messire des Chaussées will take charge of the eastern sector, between Vallans and Montamise. The seneschals under the command of Maître Lescure will take the northern sector between Montamise and Romagne. This is by far the most important terrain, but our friends are in force and we can rely on their efficiency. I myself will take the remaining front, the western sector between Romagne and Donkey Bottom. In this way the forest will be completely blockaded.

'We shall dispose of a total of six hundred men, drawn up as follows: At the rear of each column there will be positioned the knights and mounted men-at-arms from each fief, armed with lances and swords. Their particular task is to aid the escape of noble game, especially deer, which are to be allowed to pass through the lines without harm. But the horsemen will pursue and destroy all wolves and other noxious animals which may have slipped through with the game.

'The centre detachment in each force is to be the principal slaughtering body. It will consist of men-at-arms on foot operating with stakes, bows, pikes, swords and nets.

'At the head of each column will be the line of beaters armed with scythes, spears and clubs. Each will be supplied with horns, trumpets and drums, and they will advance making as much noise as possible with the object of driving the animals towards the clearing of Paix Partout in the forest heights of Paix Partout, which is the point of convergence and, according to plan, should be reached at four in the afternoon.

'Two hundred paces from Les Combles the first line will fall back to the rear of the second body, allowing the slaughterers to pass in front of them. The beaters will continue moving forward in line abreast until their flanks touch the extremities of the lines of beaters in the other columns. They will then halt, forming a square and compact hedge around the clearing. Openings in this hedge will be controlled to allow the escape of the noble game into the plain. The execution squad will, however, move slowly towards the centre of Paix Partout and exterminate all proscribed wild life: wolves, boars, badgers, bears, foxes, otters, polecats, weasels – all that noxious brood which up to this very moment is doing us such grievous harm.

'There may be beasts which, in spite of all our precautions, manage to slink through chinks in the armed fence in which we enclose them. These will be wiped out. The hunting masters of our fiefs, directing their packs of hounds, will scour all open country, field and fallow, and they will be supported by our knights and mounted men-at-arms. I require you to bring with you every available mastiff and

hunting dog to assist in the final elimination. After the main
slaughter the whole force will pass outwards through the
forest, combing it for wolf's lairs, hare's forms, fox's
earths, beaver's lodges and every burrow, den, covert, cave,
hole and haunt. Ferrets and imported terriers will be set to
this search, so that all cubs, kittens, leverets, whelps and
pups found may be destroyed. After that, God willing, we
shall bask in the peace we have so well deserved.'

A thunder of applause saluted the end of this speech.
Varlets hastened into the hall with wine so that everyone
could drink to the success of the operation. The advance
celebration went on for a long time until, dangerously late
at night, the rural warriors formed themselves into protective groups to return to their homes, or preferably slept
under the tables.

7
The Use of Heroism as Bait

Bourcet was a humble sparrow, too humble for the taste of most creatures in the forest. He was well aware of his timidity and insignificance, and his only sustenance was that, even though the going rate in the market had dropped from the times when two sparrows were sold for a farthing, he still could not fall to the ground without God knowing. He had lately been taken up by Brousse the hen-magpie. He was too well-meaning in himself to suspect that there might be a hidden motive for this. In fact, there was not: Brousse was bored with being ostracized by the forest animals after some routine piece of knavery and would have taken up with anyone she could show off to. The new crony happened to be the amiable Bourcet, and Brousse, in boredom, decided on a major demonstration of cheek. So she got Bourcet to fly with her to the castle of Crespin. She showed the sparrow how to perch and hide in the hood of the chimney of the great hall. It was a capital place for picking up gossip. They arrived during the assembly of the tenants, and they heard the whole of Messire de Frébois's fire-eating speech in the hall. The violence of the words frightened Bourcet. The menace of the wild applause appalled him. Without any of his normal hesitancy Bourcet spoke out passionately to Brousse of the danger which hovered over all his friends in the forest, and said he was going to fly straightway to warn the President of the Council, the owl Uhlan the Wise. Brousse had no option but to agree.

Uhlan nested in the great oak at La Pierre Levée by Stags Crossing. A convenient staging-post on the flight there from the castle of Crespin was La Tranchée. Brousse suggested that they should stop on the roof for a rest.

Brousse never stopped anywhere for more than a minute without making a reconnaissance sortie to see what was going on – she called it casing the joint. She came back speedily with her report. Maister Brémand had not yet returned from the meeting at the castle – as indeed could hardly be expected, unless he had come as the crow flies and without sampling his lord's wine. Dame Matilda had allowed Adèle to stay up and keep her company. They were anxiously asking each other what could be so important that the lord needed Brémand's instant attendance. Everyone else was in bed except the Flying Pig, who must have passed out with jet lag before he could stagger to his sty, for he was sprawled on a bed of dry leaves heaped in the courtyard.

'Come on down and have some fun,' said Brousse to Bourcet.

This time Bourcet hesitated, and thenceforth was lost. 'I've got a plan to save the animals,' hissed Brousse. She glanced authoritatively at Bourcet, daring him not to follow, and dropped from the roof to a spot very close to Plantagenet's snout. Bourcet shrugged, fluttered, and landed at a more respectful distance. The wind of Brousse's arrival stirred a draught of dust that made Plantagenet sneeze. He opened his eyes and recognized Brousse. He must have been dreaming of a lordly life under the influence of his fairy godmother, for he spoke very lazily, like an aristocrat.

'Dear lady! What earns me the honour of this unexpected

visit?' Plantagenet still lay on the leaves, without moving a trotter.

'An affair of the greatest importance, Squire. There are no ears here but ours and I can unload without being grassed on.' In a mixture of camp romantic diction and equally inaccurate thieves' argot Brousse gave Plantagenet a mainly faithful version of what she had overheard at the castle. As the monologue went on Plantagenet rapidly abandoned his former attitude. His uneasiness grew visibly. He laid his ears back, opened his great muzzle, put out his tongue, floundered in all directions, and alternately snorted and groaned. At the end, his haggard eyes popping out of their sockets, he let himself fall back on his bed horror-stricken, unable to make a further movement.

'Oh, come, come, Squire,' urged Brousse with her bright eyes fixed on his face. 'Pull yourself together. You're not dead yet.'

'*Dead?* Me?' gasped Plantagenet through a passable imitation of the death-rattle in his throat. 'I'm not one of the forest animals! They're not going to liquidate me too?'

'God knows what that lot are capable of,' said Brousse, delighted with the effect she was producing on Plantagenet. 'You poor innocent mug, do you think that in the heat of the action they're going to make any difference between a white pig and a black one? Not to mention that all this mob will need a lot of nourishment and there's a hue and cry for more food. Believe me, friend, if you want to get out of this with a whole skin you will have to do a bunk before Maister Brémand minces you into sausages.'

Plantagenet leapt off his death-bed and managed to stand, though his legs were shaking badly. His ears were bolt upright in his head and he was emitting faint raucous cries of terror. 'Ser ser ser,' he stammered, 'ser ser something must be done.'

'Quite right, old fellow,' said Brousse in a voice she had

to strangle to mask her secret glee. 'Ser ser certainly ser ser something must be done.'

There was a silence, which was broken only by the cackling of the hens, who could no longer restrain their curiosity and were arriving to gawp at the scene. Plantagenet tried to pull himself together, but nearly fell over in the attempt to master his shakes. The movement was enough to alarm the hens, who made off amid clattering protests that they were being victimized by a bully. Brousse saw that Plantagenet was in no state to advance the conversation and needed helping out.

'On the subject of death,' said Brousse judicially, 'I really don't see that you, old Squire, who can outrun all the animals in the forest, need incur such fatal consequences.'

Plantagenet's staring eyes slowly relaxed and he collapsed on the bed of leaves, which yielded to him with a pneumatic moan, like the sough of the wind of Hell in a far valley.

'Yes, Squire, whether you find it up your street or down the pan, destiny has chosen you to carry on your proud shoulders the safety, nay indeed, the survival of all.'

Crushed under the weight, Plantagenet buried himself a little deeper.

Brousse made rather vulgar noises in the dark as she tried to smother her giggling, and finally managed to pronounce: 'You must do your duty.'

'And how, great God?' asked Plantagenet.

Brousse, who was really a pretty awful actress, tried to register the shocked offence of an unskilled schoolmistress. Honestly, the stupidity of this pig was scraping rock-bottom. 'But after all, Squire Plantagenet, you have shared the life of these creatures for . . . how long?'

'Almost four years,' said Plantagenet blankly.

'You know their habits, their customs. You have a special sympathy with us in the forest. Of course I'm not including Hurlaud,' she added, unable to resist the spice of malice.

The mere mention of Hurlaud's name sent a shiver over Plantagenet's entire body. Brousse continued: 'Besides, you have a family there. You can't stand by and watch them be massacred. You're not aware of your own influence. Everyone in the forest likes you, you must know that.'

'Perhaps,' said Plantagenet, pleased, in a slightly firmer voice.

'You deserve their respect. You have advantages which they don't enjoy. Your wide knowledge of the outside world includes some acquaintance with the forest of Chizé, three leagues from here.'

Cheered by any suggestion that he had advantage and influence, Plantagenet was now trying out a more self-approving tone. 'That is true. So . . .?'

'Chizé is the obvious escape area. I see only one solution. We cannot pass up the chance to avail ourselves of so exceptional a leader as you. Therefore I make the following proposal.

'Bourcet!' said Brousse to the sparrow, over her shoulder without looking at him. 'Come along. Get in. Wake up. You are in on this.'

Bourcet was already growing angry at what he was beginning to hear, but was still intimidated by Brousse. He gave Plantagenet a look of deep sympathy. Then, with a sigh, he positioned himself near the magpie. After a short pause for attention Brousse continued:

'You will immediately speed to Les Combles and warn your cousin. It will be your task and his to have the alarm given and to organize a planned retreat. It will be essential that every one has somehow cleared the limits of the forest before the hunters begin their advance on it. But, since most of the animals have no idea of the shortest route leading to the forest of Chizé, it is you, Squire Plantagenet, who will lead them. I suggest that you make a rendezvous with all the animals near your cousin's place at Les Combles

next Thursday morning at seven o'clock. You can then take
the head of the column and lead them to safety.'

Bourcet was suddenly struck with horror and tried to
interrupt.

Brousse had appointed a rendezvous at seven o'clock.
That would be too late, for the hollow square of hunters
was to begin to converge from the four different quarters at
seven precisely after assembling and taking up formation
between five and seven. According to Brousse's plan the
column led by Plantagenet would reach the edge of the
forest at about nine o'clock and would then prepare to cross
the plain. At a time when they were fully exposed in the
open they would march head on into the triple line of troops
in the force led by Messire de Frébois. Inevitably there
would be a mass slaughter without the least chance of
flight. This treacherous witch of a magpie was shamelessly
betraying all those in the forest who up till then had
tolerated her behaviour as mere eccentricity. She was
planning total liquidation.

With an imperious gesture Brousse forced silence on
Bourcet. 'Let me get on, cock-sparrow. Don't fidget.'
Bourcet stuck out his beak as if he would not be gagged. 'I
must explain everything to Plantagenet in detail,' Brousse
wheedled in more honeyed tones. Bourcet weakly decided
to wait and hear the details.

'You escort the retreat to Chizé. You then come back to
this farm to pick up the news. Once the battue is declared
over you will hurry to Chizé to let everyone know. Then
you can re-form the column and lead it back in triumph to
resume occupation of the land that has always been the
proud possession of us forest folk.

'Believe me, Squire Plantagenet, you're going to make a
name from this operation above anything you've ever
dreamed of. You will be looked up to and acclaimed as our
Saviour, and recognized as the greatest and most influential

among us all. I'm not saying you're merely going to be greater than Flandrin the bear. I'm not saying greater than your cousin Grondin. I'm saying you'll be sitting at the right hand of the president of the council, greater than Hurlaud of the Great Woods himself!

'There have been complications between you and Hurlaud. I am well aware of that, Squire. Up until now you have traversed the paths from Bel Air to Malperthius or Les Combles only at speed – indeed, at very high speed. Hurlaud and his people have lain in wait for you, played you a thousand tricks, publicly mentioned their crude ambition to garnish your delicate flesh with one of their rough country sauces. You have treated them with the disdain one would expect from a gentleman of your attitude and standing. But we cannot disguise from ourselves that there has always been the possibility of a very bloody outcome.

'Now see what fate offers you: the chance to show yourself as you really are, high-minded, upright, mentally and intellectually above these ridiculous feuds, in character and temperament soaring over this pack of crude brigands. When you have completed the double heroism of leading them out into the wilderness and then back to the promised land, believe me, Squire, they'll fall down at your feet.'

Bourcet shuddered at the grossness of Brousse's flattery. He measured the magpie with his eye to see what chance he stood if he came in on Plantagenet's side. Brousse's superior muscle kept him quiet. He would never have done more than begin to hint a warning before Brousse would have torn him to pieces. Bourcet had to make the painful decision to carry his burden for some time more. But he swore to himself that he would put things right as soon as he could.

Plantagenet was a changed pig, re-invigorated and suddenly very haughty after the climax of the magpie's oratory. He was standing straight, trembling not at all, very sure of himself. He eagerly accepted the authority which Brousse was offering him, and then made gallant adieux to his visitors. Assuming with relish a lordly air, he strolled with them in a rather stilted fashion as if he had his general's commission written on a roll of parchment tucked somewhere about his person. After a few steps he turned, as if protocol would not allow him to go so far as to see them fly off, and came back thoughtfully to where he had been lying. The truth was that he had suddenly realized that he had forgotten the way to Chizé.

Try as he might, he could not reconstruct it. He had a mental block, and for a very good reason. The road to Chizé was associated with one of the most humiliating memories of his life, his acquaintance with Pommard, his quixotic notion of giving Pommard the choice of the Brémands' larder, and the buffeting he had consequently received from Maister Brémand. Even now his backside tingled at the memory.

Certainly all familiarity with the route to Chizé had been stamped out of his mind. The state of affairs therefore was that he had been appointed a military leader to conduct a planned retreat to a place he had forgotten. The appointment did not promise to be of long duration. But it had its fleeting glamour. Plantagenet departed for his sty, stalking with conscious dignity past the kennel of the suspicious Hargneu, who stared dumbfounded at such daring.

8

The Plot Thickens

Brousse had found it physically impossible to fly off from
La Tranchée. She simply had not the strength. For some
time she had been fighting back against a deep fit of the
giggles which she knew would eventually prove irrepressible.
She held on until the moment Plantagenet's back was
turned. Then she surrendered. She was absolutely out of
control. She collapsed on the damp stones of the courtyard
with her feet in the air, and she writhed with helpless
laughter. At her side, madly angry, Bourcet tried to reason
with her. 'Do you know what you've done, Madame? There
is nothing to laugh at. Plantagenet hasn't two grains of sense,
and you know it. Why drag him into such a venture? And
in particular, why have you made him fix a rendezvous at
seven o'clock when you know all the hunters will be in
position by then? What devilry are you up to?'

Brousse tried to speak, but could only spit with laughter
again. She went into convulsions. To come out of convulsions she held her claws to her belly. Her flesh was
shimmying so much with titters that she could not keep it
still with her feet and only tickled herself. This made her
laugh more. This made her lose her breath again. Finally,
between two spasms, she managed to get her message to
Bourcet. It was not benevolent.

'Idiot!' she said. 'Can't you see that this other imbecile is just the sort of stooge I need to serve my plans?' Then she fixed the sparrow very threateningly with her beady black eye. 'But make sure you don't open your beak to anyone about it, or by my oath of loyalty to and reinforcement from the First (Devil's Coven) Squadron of the Thirteenth Flying Yeomanry (The Black and Whites, Satan's Own), *you will regret it.*' Bourcet had never heard such a terrible swear. He tried to protest but the magpie had abandoned herself again to the lust for laughter. Very worried, Bourcet decided to make off – if possible, unnoticed. But the necessary strong flutter of his wings in the initial power-burst alerted Brousse. She stopped cackling long enough to screech, 'Remember the oath!' Bourcet flew away, much troubled in his mind. Brousse continued her insane staccato laughter.

'How very pleasant to meet someone in such a good mood,' said an evil voice in her ear.

The magpie stopped short, fumbled for her feet, and stood up, almost putting her head into the muzzle of the cur Hargneu. From the moist tongue of the mastiff vapour wafted lazily like steam from geyser-pools on Stromboli. But his throat puffed only the stinking blast of a volcano fed solely on carrion. Brousse had not always been on the best of terms with Hargneu. She was put out at being discovered upside down. She thought very fast to recover from her disadvantage.

'Hargneu! Just the man I was looking for! I've got a real lucky windfall for you.'

'H'm,' said Hargneu, with a paralysing blast from his interior.

Brousse called on all her extensive resources of salesmanship. 'Suppose I tell you that the battue will begin on Thursday morning at seven,' she said.

'I didn't know that. But is that the news which knocks you off your feet with amusement?'

'Suppose I tell you that all the forest animals will have decided to escape at that very time.'

'That is important. Carry on supposing.'

'Suppose I tell you that the place they will have chosen to re-form is the forest of Chizé.'

'Really?' said Hargneu. 'But that's a long trek. How will they get there?'

'I am coming to that!' shrilled the magpie. 'Suppose I tell you that they have appointed a guide who will lead them unerringly to Chizé. Suppose I tell you that this hero, the saviour of this pernicious brood, is one of your intimate acquaintances.'

'You disturb me strangely,' Hargneu uttered hoarsely. 'Tell me who it is. Let me know now, Madame, so that I can kill this traitor, this renegade, on the spot.'

'Easy, Squire! Easy does it. Don't go into action right now. It would be much wiser to listen to me without sinking your fangs into anyone, at least for the moment.' She went on, very confidentially: 'I am going to see to it that you are the hero of the occasion. All the honours will come to you. You will be first in the hunt. You will be in at the death. Too long have we, the representatives of a cultured people, been oppressed by alien barbarians who spit at our ideals of law and order. We make war only to establish peace.'

Very impressed, Hargneu sat down and cocked an ear. Brousse outlined her confident forecast of the animals' plan of escape. She named the leader. Hargneu sprang up with a bound when she identified Plantagenet. The magpie silenced him with a sharp gesture.

'There is no doubt that the heroic Plantagenet is going to march everyone on the path to Les Fosses and beyond, starting at seven in the morning. The column will need some two hours of steady marching before they reach the last clumps of trees, bordering the Guirande. Then they will have to cross the plain without any cover. That is where you will be advancing on them with the lords and commons. It is up to you – the only creature to know that they are coming – to sight them, signal them when you are indisputably ahead, and slaughter them to the last whelp.'

She finished with a short burst of oratory. 'Beasts! Brutes! Undomesticated sub-humans! It is your happy duty, my prince, to rout this rabble. I have no doubt that you will give them a very warm reception. I am particularly pleased that at last you will have the opportunity to settle all personal accounts with the wretched Plantagenet. I wish you much joy.'

Hargneu was beside himself with delight. He mouthed a torrent of endless thanks. 'Think nothing of it, my friend,' said the magpie in a lordly tone. 'On Thursday we shall be able to treat ourselves to the best laugh of our lives.'

'By my faith, Madame Brousse,' said Hargneu struggling to find a few high-flown terms on his own account, 'this is a signal service you are rendering me. Believe me, you will not find me ungrateful. Anything I can do for you in the future, dear lady, anything I can do. . . .' He groped for a suitable climax and failed. 'After all,' he declared pompously, 'what's sauce for the goose is sauce for the gander.'

Brousse made him a patronizing acknowledgement, and the two confederates separated.

9
Hark the Herald

Plantagenet spent a disturbed night planning an un-challenged break-out which would get him to Grondin in time to have the animals organized for their retreat. By the time the great gate was opened he would have only two bare days to work in. Relieving his stress, there were warmer intervals when Plantagenet let his mind wander fondly on the bliss of belonging to the forest, a claim which he could now make through his proven link with Grondin, a sworn relationship in spite of the fact that he had neither hide nor hair, black nor blemish, on his pink skin to remind anyone of his tearaway father, Grondin's uncle Tuhart. And it was a family tie which Grondin had acknowledged by actions far exceeding the demands of duty. How many times had the sight and scent of his massive black outline given Hurlaud a silent reminder that Plantagenet's hams were not on that day's menu.

Shaking his head in sentimental confusion, Plantagenet went on to think gratefully, rather in the same way that Adèle said her prayers, of Grondin's kin, of Dame Albaine who so kindly tolerated Plantagenet's permanent bewilder-ment, of the *marcassins*, young Mantan, Fartouat, and the formidable infant Pielet of the terrible teeth. And God bless all the other animals in the forest who are kind to me because they say I am polite and eager to help.

And – no harm in asking – God keep the wolves off the warpath.

Early in the morning Plantagenet buttoned on his acting personality and sauntered out of the farm enclosure. With every appearance of idleness he strolled to the edge of the forest, nosing the ground for acorns from time to time. Then he shut his eyes for a moment as if this would prevent anyone on the farm seeing him, and darted into the brushwood. His heart was pounding. His pink eyes jerked nervously about their orbit as he looked all around him for the silhouettes of Hurlaud or his brother Baclin. Plantagenet very rarely risked himself in these parts of the forest at autumn, when the cover was thin, the living was poor, and hunger drove the wolves prowling under the farm walls at night. At this time of year Plantagenet's skinny figure, however successfully it deterred the delicate humans prodding in the farmyard, was no protection against the wolves. Fifty pounds of tough gristle was still fifty pounds of useful food. When the belly yells 'Famine!' you don't flash your membership of the Gourmet Club.

Plantagenet chose what was, from the defensive point of view, the easier path through Deux Chênes. His eyes protruding, his hairs bristling, he progressed at a high speed, though not at the emergency rate which qualified him as Flying Pig. At first he tried to work out a calculation as he ran. 'If this brigand Baclin clamps on my heels *here*, or *here*, or here' – at different landmarks in the path – 'what will be the fastest way straight through the undergrowth to Les Combles?' He snorted. 'Plotting the shorter distance against the greater effort fighting thorns and creepers, I'm not within any safety margin until I reach . . . oh, I shall never do it. Step up the pace, friend,' he told himself. 'Go to the limit on the outward journey, for surely good cousin Grondin will see you back safely.'

There was a patter in the dry leaves on his starboard stern

quarter. Plantagenet was sure it was too light a step for a
wolf, but his legs threatened collapse just the same. It was
Fulgent the fox, who had seen Plantagenet on the march and
decided to give him some support by putting in a few strides
in his company.

'I see no horse-flies. What has stung you to go on the run
from La Tranchée on a day like this? You know this is
Baclin's hunting ground. Are you so tired of life?'

'Lord, no,' said Plantagenet, panting. 'But I have to see my
cousin on a matter of great importance. I have to take the
risk.'

Very discreetly, Fulgent did not pursue the matter with
questions as to what drove the pig to take such a step. This
was a very considerate display of the fox's sense of honour,
for he knew that Plantagenet, if pressed, was incapable of
keeping the least thing from him.

Plantagenet trotted on with dogged speed, and not too
delicately. Fulgent saw no point in running himself out of
breath alongside such a noisy companion. 'Go through the
gap at Pied du Fût,' he said. 'The road will be shorter. God
keep you.'

'Thanks, friend,' said Plantagenet, momentarily drawing
up his body in the most handsome manner. Then he
streaked forward and disappeared through the gap.

An hour later he crashed into the glade where Grondin
was taking his ease with his family. Exhaustion and effort
had marked the pig's body with livid patches like bruises.
The boar was startled, but did not move. Dame Albaine,
used to the eccentricities of cousin Plantagenet, made no
comment. It must be something serious that had brought
him out at such a time and in such a state. She had been
sure there was something in the wind. The deceptive quiet
of the last few days could only be the calm before a storm.
She had no illusions about Plantagenet's strongest point being
his courage, and he would certainly not have put himself

at such risk unless some exceptional event had sent him running from La Tranchée. She offered Plantagenet a place. 'Make yourself comfortable, cousin, you *are* in a state.' Plantagenet collapsed. Young Pielet snaked forward on his belly and tried a nibble at the stiff pink tail which hung at the other end of his dear uncle. Plantagenet uttered a plaintive groan.

Grondin fell on the cheeky youngster and gave him a piece of his mind: 'Leave your uncle in peace, you imp. Stretch yourself out, Plantagenet.'

The pig needed a good five minutes to get his wind back. With his tongue hanging out and his eyes glassy, he painfully came round. At last, mustering the remains of his strength, he blurted out non-stop, higgledy-piggledy with hardly a pause for breath a hotch-potch gallimaufry of the bad news and desperate remedy with which Brousse had so abundantly plied him. He spoke incoherently without continuity, his voice gradually rising as his excitement grew. Grondin did not understand a word of it, and waited patiently until his cousin came more clearly to his senses. Exhausted all over again, Plantagenet suddenly came to the end of his account, and after the torrent a heavy silence fell. Then a shaft of pain which seemed to come straight out of the earth wrung from him one last agonized shriek. The temptation had been too strong for Pielet and he had sunk his teeth in the pink tail which trailed within his reach. Grondin and Dame Albaine collided as they reared and fell on their son. His bawling added a note of intolerable shrillness to the uproar. The suffering Plantagenet felt that he had to intervene to stop his unfortunate nephew from being over-corrected. The effort straightened his own thinking. He began a new version of what he had said before, but this time he was understandable. Grondin and Albaine heard him out.

'It's what I suspected,' said Dame Albaine, very worried

but somehow relieved. She turned towards her mate.
'Haven't I been telling your lordship that something like
this was being hatched?'

'Yes, indeed, dear lady,' said Grondin with a cover of
re-assurance while he pursued his own thoughts. 'But I am
too suspicious of that shrew Brousse to believe any of her
tittle-tattle.' He made no mention of his previous encounter
with the magpie.

Plantagenet groaned. 'There's a further complication,' he
said. 'I ask for nothing better than to be the animals' guide
out of the forest through Les Fosses to Chizé. Unluckily,
and you know my weaknesses, I am not at the top of my
form. All this anxiety has affected my memory, and I can't
recall the route I must take.'

'That's nothing, cousin,' muttered Grondin, much more
absorbed in the heart of the problem than with a detail
which he judged very minor. 'I know the path well, and I'll
refresh your memory. We shall need you desperately, for
I'll have bloodier things to do.' He quickly outlined the
route, and the details revived in the pig's cloudy mind. He
began to interrupt with artless enthusiasm. 'Ah, yes, that's
it! Of course! Skirt the forest path from there as far as
Paitout. . . .' Plantagenet was happy again, almost bubbling
with gaiety. Everything he had gone through – the fearful
journey, even the mangling of his tail – dissolved in the
frothy enthusiasm of the moment like salt in cider. Grondin
grimaced indulgently at the spectacle of his ingenuous
cousin innocently revelling in such uncomplicated joy. He
reminded him gently that there was more need for reflection
than hilarity. 'Oh!' groaned Plantagenet. 'I beg pardon,
cousin. I was forgetting this wretched business. It's a long
way before we reach the outskirts of Les Fosses. Do you
think everyone amongst the animals will be able to keep up
with the column? Wouldn't it be wiser to set out as soon as
possible? Perhaps tonight?'

'No,' said Grondin firmly, having already considered the point. 'I need a clear day to muster our force and we have to march together. The mere fact of starting out together as an organized body gives us strength, and gives the weaker ones more confidence. We have also got to consider the possibility of attack. If we are chased, the operation need not go on for very long. The one thing to fear, when we are most vulnerable, will be the crossing of the plain. All the rest of the march will be done under cover. In any case we boars cannot with decency go off and leave all the others here.'

'And the dogs?' queried Dame Albaine anxiously.

'Hurlaud and Baclin and their pack will deal with them. I am going to see them immediately. No one can call them cowards, *that* you can be sure of.

'Plantagenet is coming along to see them too,' he added quietly.

Plantagenet's ears went straight up as if on springs. The names of his terrible enemies had suddenly brought back to his mind the terror of his recent journey.

'Don't agonize like that,' chaffed Grondin, who guessed the pig's concern. 'You have nothing to fear from them. Besides, we are going to see them together.'

'Oh, misery me!' groaned Plantagenet. 'I know those customers. The minute you have gone they will turn on me and chase me. I'm definitely not going. No, I think I'd better go back on my own to La Tranchée.'

'Not on your life,' said Grondin with a laugh. 'I'm telling you that they'll have other things than your hams on their minds. Come on, cousin, let's get going.'

Gasping feeble protests, far more dead than alive, Plantagenet miserably took leave of Dame Albaine and the little ones. Pielet began one more snap at his uncle's tail, but quickly sensed his misery and pretended instead to be yawning. Like a condemned man setting out for the gallows Plantagenet followed Grondin out of the glade.

10
Suspicion of Treachery

'Press on regardless!' said Grondin whimsically, keeping an amused eye on the antics of his cousin. Plantagenet, more scared than he had ever been in his life, exploding into spasm at every crackle in the undergrowth, was pressing on only in the sense that he walked with his left cheek held very tightly against the right haunch of the formidable Grondin. He went forward automatically, his tail between his legs and his eyes shut for most of the time.

'Here we are,' said Grondin, and called out in a very jovial voice, 'Bring out your dead!'

Plantagenet uttered a hoarse little cry. He took a risk and opened one eye into the narrowest possible slit. For the moment he saw nothing, but he was convinced that in the mossy heart of this fair brushwood bower before him there lurked the most hideous beast the universe had conceived. He tried to pull himself together, but no sound came from his strangled throat. He made a superporcine effort. All he could manage was a high falsetto voice which stammered thinly, 'Jollolly, jollolly, jolly good. . . . I hope.'

Suddenly an enormous grey shape glided from the thicket. There, ten paces away, was Hurlaud. His ears were

erect, his jaws were wide open, and his eyes roamed ceaselessly on the watch.

'Ah do, tha bugger?' said Grondin, meaning no offence
but using the dialect adopted by the animals for those on
'thee and tha' terms of intimacy with them. 'Hast time to
discuss a matter of some importance?' Grondin continued
very loudly.

Plantagenet felt the ground roll away under his feet.
Never had he seen the lord of this manor so close. He would
have given anything to be ten leagues away. His ears were
flat. His tail was straight and stiff rising perpendicularly from
his body. His hairs were bristling. Fear tickled at his spine.
He closed his eyes so as not to see the monster leap on him.
In his mind he could already hear his bones cracking.

'Eh, who do Ah see ba tha side? Your dear cousin?' said
Hurlaud rather comically but obviously very intent, and he
continued in a much more easy, though lordly, manner:
'Devil take you, Plantagenet, look at me. D'ye think I'm so
one-track-minded – should I say pig-headed? – to start a
fight with you here? When you pay me a friendly visit?'

Plantagenet began to tremble worse than ever. He painfully prised open one eye. He shut it immediately, green
with fear.

'Time, I think, to call a truce, bury the hatchet, lie down
with the lamb and no hard feelings,' said Grondin somewhat over-confidently. 'I fear that what's in the wind will
leave us little time for skirmishing.'

'I am very willing to believe it, Monseigneur. But come
in, come in. My home is yours to command.'

Hurlaud withdrew a little, motioning his guests to enter.
Grondin went first into the dark, warm den. Plantagenet
followed, his eyes half closed, walking as if on eggs. He felt
and smelt on his back the strong breath of the master of the
house. Little shivers ran from one end of him to the other.
Very genially Hurlaud did the honours of the house. Dame

Pernale, who was waiting inside, offered titbits and refreshments. With a tremendous effort the dazed Plantagenet managed to sit down to the right of his muscular cousin. The den was dusky but clean. To keep out the wind and the rain the brushwood lining had been tapestried with the skins of otter and sheep. In one corner, sprawling on hare skins, a litter of cubs were playing. A few bones lay on the floor, the polished relics of the Widow Bigotte's sheep. For an instant Plantagenet saw his own bones strewn around the place and another glacial shiver ran through him. Grondin made a few polite remarks and swiftly came to the point.

In a few words he outlined the news and the plan of escape which Plantagenet had brought him. Very generously he made no mention at all of his cousin's fears, but presented him as the disinterested creature he obviously was, who braved all dangers to come and give warning of the peril which hung over all. However, he expressed extreme reserve on the credibility of the report filed by the treacherous Brousse and suggested that they should try to analyse the whole situation in depth. After a long silence, broken only by the playful snarls of the cubs fidgeting on the rugs, Hurlaud said thoughtfully:

'Much of this is known to me. The manic magpie came to make her number with me this morning. I don't know why, but I smell something fishy in this doxy's behaviour. I question why she has brought your cousin into it at all. On the face of it, what does he get out of it? Why has she lured him into pioneering this retreat on our behalf? Joking apart, Plantagenet, let's face it, the folk at the castle will never make a meal out of you. Maister Brémand will have to choose a fatter pig. As for helping us, what's in it for you? It's much more in your interest to rid yourself of us sporting types who stalk you in the forest and cause you so much harassment when you're out strolling. All right, blood is

thicker than water, but you had no necessity to do more
than warn your cousin and let your intervention stop sharp
there.'

There was a fresh silence, and the wolf continued: 'No.
It's plausible but not persuasive. This trollop is putting
something over on us, Grondin, but by the blood-and-guts
of Hurlaud I swear she won't get away with it. If only we
could find an independent witness we might be able to
scratch out the truth in all this.'

Plantagenet had a sudden thought. He blushed deep at the
prospect of breaking into the conference, and then blushed
deeper with shame at not having had the thought before. He
steeled himself to speak, but at first could produce only the
high falsetto.

'There *is* a witness,' he said. 'Bourcet the sparrow was
with that slut when she called on me. It seems that both of
them were hiding in the castle chimney.'

'*That's important*,' roared Hurlaud and Grondin at the
same time, and they asked Plantagenet to go word by word
through what Brousse had had to say without leaving a
thing out. Plantagenet started, hesitantly at first, but
gradually his feeble voice gained assurance and he let himself go, narrating all the details.

'It's essential that we find Bourcet,' said Hurlaud energetically. 'A rather timid bird, I fear. Not one of my
admirers. I can't see him giving very illuminating verbals
if I'm opposite him. Which is why, Grondin, I suggest that
it's up to you to fix a rendezvous at the beech in Pré Vinet,
which is where the dear midget has his pad. You're a great
inspirer of confidence. He'll come across to you. What do
you say, Monseigneur?'

'I can only hope,' said Grondin. 'But, not knowing
whether he'll talk or not, we have to make emergency plans.
It is of top urgency to consult with Uhlan the Wise but,
really, everyone must have immediate warning.' Grondin

mentioned the names of all those in the forest who, from
the human side of the indictment, had a little mayhem on
their record and should therefore discreetly flit. Hurlaud
added other names of his own acquaintance. Between them
they drew up a complete list of all those who could expect
to be proscribed.

When they had finished Hurlaud efficiently chaired the
meeting to a close. 'First I am going to have a talk with my
brother Baclin,' he said. 'There are one or two matters that
I want to agree with him. There are other tasks that you and
I have to complete, Monseigneur Grondin. We have to see
that everyone is summoned to a Council – I think Les
Combles would be convenient. But first we fix the time for
it with Uhlan the Wise. Then we can call the Council. Of
course we shall have to get a message through to Plantagenet.
I very much hope he will be present and make a full state-
ment so that all the animals know the extent of the crisis.
I shall work on the organization of the retreat immediately
but I see already that one condition is essential: we must set
out at five in the morning and not at seven. We must have a
reserve of time. The little ones, the young boars and the
wolf cubs of this year's litter won't be able to keep up the
pace. I'm not worried about what will happen at the other
end. You and we' – he was referring to the boars and the
wolves – 'still have some relatives at Chizé and certainly on
our side we keep in touch with them from time to time.'
Hurlaud smiled warmly at Dame Pernale, who was pleased
to acknowledge his salute. 'Between relatives and friends
and common goodwill to creatures in trouble we shall be
fed and quartered decently for some time.'

Grondin nodded, grunted, and beamed with satisfaction
like a corpulent eastern Sultan aware that he can entrust
State business unhesitatingly to his wily Vizier. He rose
ponderously from his reclining position, putting the
tapestried bush walls of the wolf's den in temporary peril.

'That's just how I see it,' he said. 'I'm delighted with what we have achieved in our conference. Come, cousin. I will see you home.' Grondin bowed to Dame Pernale and bade a less formal farewell to Hurlaud with, 'Good neet, tha bugger.'

'Good neet, tha bugger,' said Hurlaud with a slight contraction of his lean and aristocratic, if cynical, face that might equally have indicated winking or wincing. Then he spoke very graciously to Plantagenet. 'I have been much honoured by your visit, Plantagenet,' he said with an inclination of his head and a small flourish that seemed totally serious, not to be mistaken for play-acting. 'I greatly appreciate your offer of help, and, believe me, it will be very precious to us all.' Plantagenet stammered some words of thanks and turned to go out of the den with, this time, his tail under full control slung decently low and ringed, and his ears turned proudly to the wind. He breathed deeply as he came into the fresh air, not in emotional relief but, since the truth had to be faced, to take a draught of tonic after his spell in close company with a family of flesh-eaters whose breath was . . . somewhat strong. The fact remained that, for every conceivable reason, emotional and physical, Plantagenet felt rather pleased with himself.

Grondin benevolently escorted his cousin to the edge of the clearing opposite La Tranchée. He stopped a few paces short of the last of the trees and took leave of Plantagenet with the farm wall well in sight.

'I'll try and get a message to you to warn you of the time of the meeting, but it will not be easy. I suggest that you should have in mind that it may be at Les Combles at about five tomorrow night. That's when I think the big decisions will be made, on the time of the exodus next morning. I cannot even begin to convey to you how deeply we are all in your debt. Thank you, cousin Plantagenet.'

He stood for a moment, his black bulk towering over the

diminutive porker. Then, enormous, majestic, and with his usual complete disregard for stealth, he turned and went back into the forest, the deadwood snapping like whip-cracks under his indifferent feet.

Plantagenet, who had withstood a whole swarm of ordeals and emotions that day, found himself alone, opposite the farm – and reality? For a moment he stood still, savouring the silence of this forest where, for the most part unseen, a whole order of wild life regulated its existence with considerable freedom and more than a trace of nobility. He told himself that Hurlaud, in intelligence and manners, had much of the air of the grand seigneur and that, if all due account was paid to wolves, they were as good in their own world as the human wolves shut up within the shelter of their walls. Which world, then, was Plantagenet's? What animal was he to be? At the moment he felt himself more at one with the creatures of the forest. He had found more dignity there than any animal, slave or free, had ever before accorded him. Who among even the most arrogant of animals could boast alongside the pig Plantagenet that he had sat for some time in the den of Hurlaud of the Great Woods, and had come out with honour? What a presence that animal had! What a difference from the beasts whom Plantagenet had run with! How free he clearly felt himself! How sure of himself he was! Plantagenet smiled as he thought of his companions within the farm, who bent their backs and sweated under harness. But his smile was one of affection. He went out into the open and, stumbling a little through fatigue, he passed through the great farm porch.

11
Action by the Prince of Darkness

Immediately Plantagenet came into the main courtyard he glimpsed the scurry of a white dress from the house and saw Adèle running towards him. 'Plantagenet, where have you been?' she asked, not scolding but seeming happy and wanting to share. Her cool fingers kneaded his shoulder. 'A good wandering brother has been here,' she said, 'but he would not stay, only he talked to me as I gave him a meal. He was telling me of his sweet sister Clare and I wanted him to meet my brother Plantagenet. And he told me of his brother Masseo who called on heaven and was given the grace of humility, and ever afterwards was so happy that as he prayed he would make a glad sound like the deep cooing of doves. I told him how strange that was, for when I am happy I pipe like a woodlark in song-flight with a toolooeet lu-lu-lu-lu. But perhaps brother Masseo is different because he is a man and his voice has broken, which mine never will. Now Plantagenet, you must be a good brother and if you don't want to provoke people you must keep out of the way, for everything is confusion here. And I am very busy myself, so I must fly, though not really fly like a woodlark.' And she soared back to the house singing, 'Toolooeet lu-lu-lu-lu.'

There was indeed remarkable confusion at La Tranchée. Maister Brémand had come home from Castle Crespin and had set the whole farm by the ears. He knew that the lords would stop at his place after the hunting operation and he was determined that they should find the house in good order while they emptied a few crocks of wine. He ordered that the leaves should be piled, the carts carefully lined up in the sheds, the ploughshares scraped clean and shining and the courtyard should be swept, so that everything should be spotless. It was the same inside the house, where Dame Matilda and Adèle and the servants washed the floors, polished the furniture and burnished the copper.

In the courtyards men were busy all over the place, currying the horses and setting up the wagons. One washed the dogs, energetically showering them with buckets of water and pummeling them with sponges. Hargneu had found himself included in this operation. Usually hopelessly daubed with thick field mud, he had suddenly emerged as a changeling in a black and white coat. Water was entirely disagreeable to him, and he could perceive no gentleness in the calloused hands which brushed him remorselessly, but occasionally one must suffer to be beautiful.

All this bustle had caused some distress in the lower courtyard. Lancet the cock desperately tried to gather his hens around him as they dashed about, cackling in panic. It soon became clear that the only place which had so far escaped the frenzied activity was Plantagenet's sty, to which the pig had swiftly retired and promptly slumped into slumber. The good-natured Plantagenet had always made it clear that harassed exiles were sure of a welcome if they contemplated a short stay in his domain, and his farm companions could treat the pig-sty as open house. With this in mind the chickens, geese, guineafowl, and even Sobrin the donkey, who were all anxious to avoid a wash, stalked to their refuge in a body, posting one hen outside as a look-out. In a moment the pig-sty became a Noah's Ark with all the nervous inmates giving free vent to their annoyance, particularly the hens, who kept up a disapproving running commentary on all the hullabaloo outside. 'My dear, have you seen what a mess all this washing makes? All I ask is Why?'

'I swear I've never seen such commotion. If the Pope himself had deigned to visit the Master one could not have been put to more trouble.'

Plume the goose ventured a joke at the donkey's expense: 'Sobrin, you're filthy. At least you ought to go and have a lick and a promise. You're sure to be chosen as the herald to bray a welcome when the lords arrive.'

'Silence, ladies, *if* you please!' crowed Lancet without any hope of success. 'Our host is asleep.'

'Pooh, asleep!' answered Plume with some bitterness. 'This layabout gets out of everything, including his duty to his master. Brémand can't even put him up for supper for the lords. They'd certainly get short commons.' This remark proved highly amusing to many among the obstreperous guests and they cackled loudly with mirth. Plantagenet lazily opened an eye.

'No one can say anything of the sort about you, dear lady,' he observed. 'You are as plump and as tender as could be wished. You don't know how glad I am that my flesh is so much less desirable than yours. Take my advice. Don't hang around too near the kitchen.'

He opened the other eye. 'What on earth is going on? I just take a few minutes' doze after a little saunter and I wake in the middle of bedlam. Isn't there one of my friends with the courage to say Boo to a goose?' Plume retired in utter defeat. The others cackled just as loudly in appreciation of Plantagenet as they had recently done for Plume.

Sobrin the donkey showed signs of mild alarm. 'I should

have thought,' he said gently, 'that the best way to persuade people to forget our existence is not to remind them of it. In a word, keep quiet.'

'Two words,' snapped Plume.

Sobrin continued in a voice as good-humoured as before but with his eye roving over Plume with a butcher's calculation: 'Why must it always be those most at risk who signal most wildly to Atropos, the last and gravest of the Fates, that it is time to cut the thread?' At this remark there was a general silence, and then the rustle of the stretching of feathered bodies, as the poultry drew themselves up in order to decrease their bust measurements, and then drew themselves down to diminish the length of their necks.

Plantagenet whispered a suggestion to Sobrin. 'All right,' said Sobrin. 'You are not as foolish as people think you are. God hold you in his holy keeping.'

'My friends,' announced Plantagenet, 'I'm going to scout for some news. Stay here quietly and wait for me.' And he went out into the courtyard.

Hardly had he turned the corner of the henhouse when he came upon a strange new animal, very black where he was black, very white where he was white, shining like a painted rocking-horse. The mouth opened in a hideous grimace displaying two appalling rows of teeth, and Hargneu had disclosed his identity. Plantagenet, still dizzy with the glamour of his recent welcome in the forest, was unimpressed. 'Pah!' he told himself. 'I've seen better than that. I wouldn't put my shirt on those ickle toothypegs if they were deployed in a battle with Hurlaud. Hargneu, my old bonzo, you're not in the big league. Cultivate a little modesty and stick to rat-catching.' And muttering in this manner Plantagenet paraded past the dog with his head high, dirty but disdainful.

Because of his special status the pig had the run of the house and he went towards the door. It was closed, and the

uproar on the other side did not seem at all inspiring.
Plantagenet turned away, and suddenly found himself face
to face with Edmond, the oldest of the varlets.

'Ah, my good fellow,' said Edmond. 'It's not your day,
doncherknow. Mamselle Adèle is very busy. Everything
must be spotless, you see. And that must include you.'
With one bound he seized Plantagenet by the ears and the
tail, and threw him into a butt of cold water. Mad with
rage, Plantagenet floundered in the flood, emphasizing his
allegations of violation with the most raucous cries.
Nothing came of them. He was held, dunked, soaped,
brushed, rinsed and finally curried with a scrubbing brush,
all under the mocking eye of the ruffian Hargneu. As soon
as Plantagenet came out of that cursed tub he had but one
fixed idea, to get back to his sty and go deep in the straw. He
held himself in, not wanting to display the depths of his
distress in front of Hargneu. But soon the cur, casting a
look of superior scorn at Plantagenet, went away to go
prowling behind the kitchen.

Immediately, using the tension of his suppressed anger
like a spring, Plantagenet shot from the hands of Edmond,
who was still crooning with delight at the beautiful job he
had done. The sty was not far away, and nothing would have
pleased Plantagenet more than to have dived under the
straw, where it would take exceptional cunning to uproot
him. But his friends were still in the sty, and to make his
escape there would only draw attention to them. He could
never forgive himself if one or other of them paid with their
life solely because he had led the slaughterers to their hide-
out. Since he could not retreat because of his scruples, the
only alternative was some dramatic action which would at
least demonstrate his displeasure: The Pig Plantagenet Was
Not To Be Treated Like That. Nor was he to be Looked
At Like That, Spoken To Like That, nor Laughed At Like
That. All these unfriendly actions were going on at that

very moment. In spite of the look of bitter hatred which Plantagenet was trying to focus on him, old Edmond was guffawing and gasping between chuckles: 'What a lovely looking stripling you've turned out to be, Plantagenet. Itty-bitty-diddums, you must have been a beautiful baby. A real sugar-plum, doncherknow. If only you'd oblige by putting on a few dozen pounds, we should be getting a taste of your hams at Easter.'

This was too much. Plantagenet saw a tub full of soot from the chimney, which had just been swept in the fury of house-cleaning. He charged the butt, overturned it, and rolled over and wallowed in the soot with the deepest satisfaction until the skin which Edmond had scrubbed so white was as black as a charcoal-burner's.

Edmond's howls of protest, and the idiot laughter of the other varlets, caught the attention of Maister Brémand, who was passing near. But when he saw Plantagenet he had to join in the general mirth. He tried to trot out some saw of country wisdom to console the discomfited Edmond: 'Edmond, you ought to understand that Plantagenet is teaching us a valuable lesson. What's bred in the bone will out in the flesh, pearls before swine, chip off the old block, better my hog dirty home than no hog at all.' He stared at Plantagenet thoughtfully for a moment and said: 'I do believe this chap has a bit of the boar in his blood. If only he were a little bigger you could well credit it.' He went affectionately towards Plantagenet, who was enjoying a mood of quiet satisfaction after his outburst and did not retreat.

'Stay black, old fellow, if that's what you want,' said Maister Brémand, and he dipped down into the soot and rubbed it in wherever the skin was still white. 'Let him be, Edmond, you can't fight nature,' he said.

'Ah, good master, this beast will turn your brain,' said Edmond reproachfully.

'Perhaps he is wiser than any of us,' said Brémand with a smile, and then he jumped to hustle the other varlets who had stopped to watch the interlude, or had profited from the diversion to take a few minutes' rest in the barn.

Plantagenet was left alone, admiring himself from tip to tail. Never had he been so black. He felt as brave as a boar already. In self-conscious majesty he strode back to the sty. He crossed the threshold and ran straight into a wave of fright and hostility. Sobrin carefully put the correct distance between himself and the intruder and launched a kick of which only donkeys have the secret. Plume uttered a series of shrill squawks which were immediately taken up by all the hens. A battery of beaks darted towards Plantagenet like pikes.

'What fine friends I have,' said Plantagenet sulkily. 'I leave the place for a moment and they bar me from my own home.'

'Plantagenet!' brayed Sobrin, 'is it really you?'

'Who else?' said Plantagenet. 'Who do you think I am? The Devil in person?' The huddle of feathers at the end of the sty relaxed slowly into the shapes of identifiable poultry. Plombe the guineafowl stretched out a neck to breathe the familiar smell of Plantagenet, but could not distinguish it. Only the voice gradually convinced everyone that this was their host.

'You gave us a good fright,' said Lancet striding angrily back and forth. 'And what's the point of this disguise? Do you fear for your life? Is this the only way you can get out of going on the menu?'

'No,' said Plantagenet as a sudden thought struck him. 'But wait a minute, my friends. Keep your eyes peeled if you want to give yourselves a good laugh.' And without any further explanation he slipped out of the sty.

A mischievous idea was dawning in his mind. If his friends, of all people, had found it so hard to recognize him there was a strong chance that this hooligan Hargneu would come a cropper. There was an old account to settle with Comrade Hargneu. There had been another unsolicited bath, in a stinking cess-pool, which brought back nauseating memories. Worms turned, biters were bit. Even a mild and genial pig, brother to Adèle and all doves, could occasionally be fired to follow the sombre lustre of the star of Vengeance.

Opportunity bowed to him. But he still needed discretion. If he suddenly revealed himself to the dog and chased him, both of them would immediately be chased, not only with the revelation of the truth, but with cudgels. He must find a moment to corner the enemy in a deserted spot, and above all to wait after setting a trap.

Very cautiously Plantagenet skirted two farm servants who were climbing a high ladder on Brémand's orders to re-wash in white lime the wooden lean-to extension to the fowlhouse. Balancing their pails and brushes, they were too encumbered to notice the dark shape which sneaked through a back door into the larder and came out again almost immediately holding in its jaws a huge sausage which it had just liberated. Making sure that he was not noticed, Plantagenet scampered at speed round the lean-to and deposited the sausage in full view near a heap of hay that had fallen there by chance.

The place was nicely deserted. The pig glided into the nearby barn. Vigorously tossing his snout, he made himself a comfortable hide-out, his body completely hidden under the hay, with a tiny peep-hole for observation. He settled down to wait.

He waited. He waited. He fought off the insidious temptation to doze, while Hargneu spun out the suspense. Evening began to deepen. Soon the courtyard glowed with that shifting magic light – now you see things, now you don't – which clears and obscures like breath on a window before the curtain swiftly falls and it is Night. Outside, the men working on the lean-to were debating whether they should work on by candle-light.

Then suddenly a curious form came round the corner. It was shaped like a dog. It had four legs, but for much of the time it used only three, tucking the right fore-leg in after every two or three paces as it made elaborate bows to right and left, like a horse in a circus. It seemed to do nothing but smile, if a contrived baring of a dog's teeth can be called a smile. Occasionally it stopped strutting and lovingly licked selected areas of its hide, which was clear black-and-white even in the dusk. It was Hargneu, luxuriating in the rare glory of a clean skin.

Forgetting his disguise and his secret observation post, Plantagenet yielded to an unexpected reaction and shrank as low as possible in his niche in the hay.

Hargneu came on without a care in the world. As he came by the barn he passed in front of the pile of hay without giving it a glance.

Plantagenet frothed with rage and frustration.

Suddenly the dog made a half-turn and fell from the rear on the bait, of which he had been aware for several seconds. His mouth filled with saliva. This was an unexpected windfall. No doubt in the general confusion of the evening a servant had been carrying food to the stock-pile for the planned banquet, and had accidentally dropped the sausage. Hargneu gave a cautious glance to right and left, and suddenly seized the object of his lust and began to devour it on the spot.

He found the first taste quite superb. While he was concentrating on the savour Plantagenet, with a quiet grace more wolfish than swinish, cautiously slank from his hiding place to a position just behind Hargneu. At this moment Blanche the black hen appeared at the farther end of the barn, sent on a sortie by Sobrin to catch a glimpse of what was going on. A menacing growl from the dog saluted the hapless hen, who fled at once in fright.

Hargneu was at the height of ecstasy. Man, this meal was good! What expertise the Masters had, what skill, to preserve meat like this and let it mature through the months, improving all the time.

Hargneu felt breath drifting over his back.

He took no notice at first. Then he felt the breath again. He turned round in rage at being disturbed. And suddenly his fury faded. Opposite him, reeking with unmistakable menace, was – a boar. Plantagenet, his hairs all bristling, his cheeks puffed and his eyes half-closed, had practically doubled in size. He was fulfilling his rôle perfectly.

'Oh mamama Monseigneur!' stuttered Hargneu. 'Fancy sususu surprising people like that!'

'I have come to pay you a little visit,' said Plantagenet, managing to deepen the pitch of his voice.

'Nanana naturally I'm very honoured,' said the dog. 'But why come here?'

'Because it's important. And it can't wait,' said Plantagenet darkly, and he made a forward movement. Hargneu leapt sideways, but Plantagenet, moving with impressive speed, had barred his way. A fluttering thrill ran through a spellbound audience beyond the pair, where all the inhabitants of the lower courtyard, plus the donkey Sobrin, had packed the front stalls to see the show.

'Don't bother to bunk, Bonzo,' growled Plantagenet. 'You wouldn't get far.'

'What do you want from me?' stammered Hargneu, still guarding the half-eaten sausage between his paws.

'Do you know the pig Plantagenet?'

'Oh, yes,' smirked Hargneu. 'You mean the swine who lives at this farm?'

'He's no friend of yours, apparently.'

'An acquaintance. We see each other from time to time,' said Hargneu vaguely. 'Passers-by. . . .'

'Liar!' roared Plantagenet. 'You don't pass him, you persecute him. I know it, d'you hear me? He has told me.' Very deliberately he strode two paces forward and prodded his snout into the dog, who was now too scared to run. The tension in the audience was electric. This cur was going to find out at last what life was all about.

'He must have made a mistake, a big mistake,' groaned Hargneu, glancing sideways at the pile of hay to judge what protection it might offer. 'I don't wish him the least harm, Monseigneur.'

'Shut up, you stinking mongrel,' ordered Plantagenet. 'Before your guts shrivel in the winter wind through this courtyard you're going to hear a thing or two from me. I am Plantagenet's cousin, do you understand? He is of the same blood as me. I am Grondin the boar. How many times have I had to listen to the pleas of this poor pig, a creature so gentle in his nature and so good to you all. How many times has he had to come to me at my home to ask protection. I have seen him bitten and bloody, driven to my lair to plead with me to save him from you, because you are his bullying tormentor. I am Grondin, do you understand? And now in front of all this congregation assembled here you are going to confess your miserable guilt, or I'll split your belly open with one snap.'

Hargneu could not believe his ears. How could it happen that this puny Plantagenet had the courage to venture into the deep woods as far as Les Combles, let alone the gall to get this brute Grondin to raid the very farm where Hargneu lorded it in full security? The dog's eyes turned up with terror. He howled before he was hit, in the hope that he could attract attention. 'Aie, aie, Monseigneur,' and he prolonged the howl to increase the effect. 'I confess. I confess everything. But for mercy's sake don't take what he has told you too literally. I've sometimes thumped Plantagenet and played him a trick or two, but I never. . . .'

'Buzz that for a tale,' yelled Plantagenet with mounting rage. 'Thumped? Tricks?'

'Aie, aie! Yes, I have beaten him up. I have even wished him dead. I. . . .'

He did not finish. Plantagenet the boar pounced on the dog. He seemed to have borrowed ten times his normal strength from the cousin whose name he had taken. He savaged Hargneu, ripped him, dragged him in the mud, gave him the old one-two with left-right crosses from his whizzing snout, and left the dog half-stunned in the mire.

'Help! I'm dying!' shrieked Hargneu in desperation, and in a last leap of energy he managed to free himself and flee, howling with terror. He did not forget, however, to snatch up the remains of his dinner. Plantagenet hurled himself at the retreating warrior and lodged one last bite on his tail. But as soon as the brace of racers reached the corner of the cow-shed Plantagenet abandoned pursuit, leaving Hargneu to continue his demented flight, bawling with all his being. Darting down the passage by the side of the lean-to which the farm servants were lime-washing, Hargneu crashed head-on into the bottom of the ladder. As the dog took the contents of the paint-bucket on his back, one of the men fell and the other stayed clutching the gutter and shouting for help. Thinking that the shouts came from pursuers, Hargneu burst straight into the cow-shed, shrieking the curious alarm which can be sounded only by a dog with a sausage in its jaws. Understandably disturbed, the cows first overturned the milk-buckets and then the milk-maids, stove in the only available door, and departed bellowing into the courtyard. Almost crushed by the cows' hooves and the maids' clogs, Hargneu decided to take another exit, and disappeared into the privies. The first legs he hit were those of Maister Brémand.

'Brute! Scoundrel! Good-for-nothing! Thief!' roared
Maister Brémand holding his breeches in one hand and a
handy spade in the other, and he chased the dog as fast as he
could. 'Look at him! Chase him! He still has what he stole
in his mouth. Get Pierre down from that gutter. Put the
ladder back. Help me with my breeches. I'm going to murder
him!' And, running now a little faster, he made after
Hargneu.

'MURDER him?' shrieked Dame Matilda, suddenly rising
in his path like a banshee. 'We can't afford to kill him. It
brings bad luck on the house, and this is no time for the evil
eye. For Nick's sake, don't kill him, the brute is still young
and there are years of work in him yet.'

'Tie him up, Edmond,' said Maister Brémand, breathing
hard. 'Tie him up tight, just a little short of breaking his
neck.' He went back to the lean-to which the men had been
liming. 'Nothing wrong with you? You'll live. Oh, well,
it's just bad luck. Enough excitement for one evening,
friends. Let's go in to supper.'

And with great strides, and a hint of a laugh in his eyes,
Brémand crossed the courtyard and led the way into the
kitchen, adjusting his dress as he strode.

12

Interrogation of a Witness

During the last restless day before the battue the beagle Rupert, idling in the brushwood, ran across Fulgent the fox. For reasons connected with their mutual dislike of the farmer Henriot they had long ago concluded a pact of non-aggression. Naturally Rupert told Fulgent of what he called the priceless how-di-do, Plantagenet's trick against Hargneu. The fox retailed the story to Grondin, and there was high amusement throughout the forest.

'What a rogue Plantagenet is becoming,' Grondin told Fulgent between bellows of laughter. 'And any fright he can start at this time is useful.'

'Yes, but they're working on their own project,' said Fulgent. 'It's no secret at La Tranchée that it's D-Day tomorrow. Have you warned everyone in your section of the Wanted List?'

'Yes. They will all be ready except Pasquin the badger, whose family is too young. He thinks he'll never manage the crossing of the plain with his brood. He has no intention of leaving Dame Vibiette alone with them, and he proposes to dig in here and stay underground. He tells me he has dug three extra tunnels and has collected enough provisions to stand a siege.' Grondin paused, reflected a little, and added quietly: 'It is very serious, with the prospect of ferrets as well as dogs.'

All the animals were tense and excited as they prepared their exodus. Dame Brousse, delighted to see her scheme materializing, flew from place to place squandering her advice on every one and emphasizing the seven-o'clock start. Very few knew of her treachery, and those who did kept grimly silent. From the moment when the lords of the wolves and the boars had taken their decision with Plantagenet every available animal had been alerted by Hurlaud, Baclin, Fulgent or Grondin.

As he had agreed, Grondin went to Pré Vinet to look for Bourcet the sparrow. He easily located him, curled up in his nest in a fork halfway up a beech. 'Bourcet,' Grondin shouted, 'come down. I have some things to ask you which there is no point in anyone else hearing.' Grondin hoped that Bourcet would catch the allusion to Brousse, who was quite likely to be nosing around somewhere near, keeping an eye on Bourcet to make sure the sparrow held his tongue.

After some hesitation Bourcet extricated himself from his ball of moss and dropped a few feet to perch on a main branch of the tree. 'Lower down, Bourcet, lower down. You're not pretending you don't know me?' said Grondin in a superior manner which was intended to convey to the sparrow the boar's keen disapproval of any lack of trust.

'Yes, of course, Monseigneur, I know you very well,' said Bourcet. 'And I have no recollection of anything that may have come between us unless it was that acorn which I liberated from under your nose last week.'

Grondin began to laugh, a little artificially. 'Ah, you jolly young scrounger, you have a long memory. I never gave the matter another thought. A little thing like an acorn! You liberated it, of course, liberated it. Who said you pinched it? You must understand I sometimes seem a little out of temper, and don't take kindly to scrumping going on right under my nose. Much less kindly,' added the boar, who had clearly been giving the matter rather more than another thought, 'much less kindly when I had taken a lot of trouble to dig up that particular acorn myself. . . .'

'Point taken,' the sparrow interrupted hurriedly. 'As you said, I didn't pinch it.'

'No, dear friend, of course not,' said Grondin in as conciliatory a manner as he could muster. 'One acorn for you is a windfall. It gives you something to nibble at all day, perhaps two days. . . . As far as I'm concerned I need a few pounds.'

'Then it was hardly worth while swearing at me as you did,' said Bourcet, with the mixed influences of tears and resentment both sharpening his voice.

Grondin looked abashed. The truth was that he was not very proud of having abused this inoffensive bird who was so well-meaning that even Fouisset the polecat had spared him so far. Softening to the crestfallen repentance being offered below him, Bourcet flew down and perched very near Grondin's nose. 'Let's make it up, dear friend,' said Grondin. 'What I have come to ask you is of vital importance to all of us here. I have seen Plantagenet.'

'Ah!' said the bird, jumping up and settling one hop farther away. 'He has told you?'

'Yes. And we think that in this report which Plantagenet has given us in so much detail there is one fact that lacks the ring of truth. That is the exact time of the battue.'

Bourcet twisted like a worm. He would willingly have told Grondin the truth, but the memory of Brousse's threats to him weighed on his mind and froze him into silence. Grondin had guessed this, and he went on to say in an offhand manner:

'The battue will be dangerous for you, too. Your nest is not all that high. One casual hoist of a lance and you could well be spitted on the point of it. Why not come to Les

Combles? You will be safe there. Once we have gone off you will be free to stay a few days with Uhlan the Wise. It will be a bold creature, creeping or flying, who manages to bring off any grievous bodily harm on you once you're under Uhlan's wing.'

'Creeping or flying, you say, Monseigneur. Any GBH I get lumbered with will definitely be airborne. I take it you comprenny the person to whom I'm alluding. I don't fancy facing her pointed beak whether I'm in the fortifications of Crespin or taking sanctuary with Uhlan. She has ordered me to keep silent. If I let you in on it she will pay me out one day or another.'

'But Bourcet, you are under the protection of all the forest. I am giving you this assurance on the word of Hurlaud of the Great Woods and of his brother Baclin. If this termagant comes near you, no matter how far away we are at the time, she will have us to deal with. One further item of news which may interest you is that Bafrin the falcon and Puissard the sparrowhawk are wholeheartedly on your side and they are dying to give Brousse a taste of real aerial combat, and I do mean the genuine article. You have nothing to fear from anyone, and I shall make a formal announcement to the Council that you are under our protection.'

Beaming with new confidence at this reassurance, Bourcet let himself go, narrating all that had happened when he was hidden in the chimney of the great hall. 'Five o'clock, five o'clock, Monseigneur, is the hour of the rendezvous. By seven o'clock the troops will be closing in. If you leave the forest at seven, as Brousse has been planting in everyone's mind, there is no way in which you'll dodge falling into their hands.'

'That is what I suspected, old friend, and Hurlaud was even more convinced than I was. I thank you in the name of all of us. Now what about leaving these digs and coming

over to Les Combles? I shall be busy with all the arrangements that have still to be made, but Dame Albaine and
Puissard will take care of you.'

'Are you quite sure that Puissard . . . ?'

Grondin nearly blew up, but he managed to restrain himself. This tiny fluff of feathers was nothing but a bundle of
suspicion. He stared fixedly into the two little balls of jet
which were the sparrow's eyes.

'Now, Bourcet, if I say a thing. . . .'

At that moment, skimming the top of the beech, Brousse
flew over the two confederates on a reconnaissance. 'Hurry
up, Bourcet,' said Grondin. 'She's watching you. I have to
go now and make ready for the meeting that has been called.
Do me a favour, cut along, and if you are in need of anything tell Dame Albaine that I can be found at Hurlaud's.'

He gave the sparrow no further time for reflection, but
went purposefully off. Bourcet chirped some more-than-
formal thanks at his departing tail, and flew off towards Les
Combles.

13
A Fighting Retreat is Ordered

The Grand Council of the Forest had been called for that time in the afternoon when the clear glade of Les Combles still glowed, even in autumn, with a steady light: Plantagenet's favourite hour between Nones and Vespers – but Plantagenet could not get to the meeting. Hurlaud and Baclin had whipped in much of the attendance, with the indispensable help of Fulgent the fox, who was not only nimble and speedy but extremely knowledgeable: he knew where everyone hung out; the tiniest dens in the most secluded corners of the forests had had Fulgent canvassing at the entrance.

Baclin had found time to visit Uhlan the Wise and put him in the picture. The Grand Old Owl had grasped the importance of the crisis in a trice, had consented to the extraordinary meeting of the Council, and had sent Bafrin the falcon on an urgent mission to Chizé where he was to find Rohart, a cousin of Grondin, and organize with him the temporary lodging and entertainment of the emigrants. Bafrin had gone off like an arrow without waiting to make sure that he could get back to Les Combles by the time of the meeting. But he could be relied on to do his best to bring a reply from Rohart in time. Rohart and Uhlan were old friends, and in times of emergency remedies were fixed faster and more reliably if the negotiations were left to the old clan heads who at other times were perhaps regarded as doddering.

Bafrin the Noble was a natural-born solitary hero. He was well known for diving headlong straight into farm courtyards to pluck up a hen or a guineafowl amid the curses and the crudely-levelled weapons of the peasants working around. He had brushed with death on many occasions, but never as a poseur pretending that he had a contempt for life. The great Hurlaud always talked of him with respect. Although he was by temperament an individualist, Bafrin the Noble had never hesitated to expend his strength to the limit and to run any risk if it was for the common good. He lived unsociably, nesting in the dead willow at Casse Tombereau. He was a true member of the circle of the Hurlauds, the Baclins, the Fulgents, the Grondins and their kind. When his eye flashed with the piercing gleam of the predator, there was assurance that he knew how to make himself respected. The story was told that once, when he had taken a hare for himself, Baclin pounced and disputed it with him. There was a bitter fight, but the falcon did not yield his prey, and Baclin lost so much blood from the bird's stabbing beak that he was forced to retreat. This was the sort of tale told in the forest that put a misty halo of glory round Bafrin's image.

While the falcon sped on his mission to Chizé the Grand Council met in the clearing at Les Combles.

Among those present were:

Grondin the boar and Dame Albaine, his companion;
Baclin de Saint Symphorian Souligné and his Lady;
Hurlaud des Grands Bois and Dame Pernale;
Bursiat the boar (a distant relative of Grondin) and his herd;
Fulgent des Saules the sinuous king-fox, as much at home

and at ease by the river as were the willows from which he
drew his title;

Fléton, brother to Fulgent, with Tibelle his Dame;

Pasquin the badger and Dame Vibiette;

Flandrin the bear and his brothers;

Nucille the otter and her companions;

Fouisset the polecat;

Dame Pernisse the weasel with all her family;

Puissard the sparrowhawk;

with many other family members of the clans represented,
all conversing in little groups beyond the coverts before
moving to take up their positions around Hurlaud des
Grands Bois and Uhlan le Sage.

The meeting was remarkably quiet, although never in
living memory had so many attended such an assembly. All
the breeds which could expect to fear the destructive hand
of man were represented in a free parliament of those wild
creatures who chose to keep only the forest law, even when
it challenged the customs of man and his intolerable itch to
subdue.

Hurlaud had carefully contrived that the meeting should
take place in the greatest secrecy by a simple reliance on the
instinct of self-preservation, reserving attendance only for
those who were soon likely to endure the precisely calculated butchery of Messire de Frébois and his tacticians.
It had been essential to keep the magpie Brousse isolated
from the action, since with a few strokes of her wings she
could waft and report the conclusions of the conference to
every pack of hounds in the district. To evade what would
have been virtual genocide a simple subterfuge had been
concocted. Lupiot, the multi-coloured hedge-rat, had been
commissioned to tickle the fancy of the feathered floozy
and keep her talking till twilight. To help Lupiot in a task
which was doubly difficult, from the point of view of
enduring her malicious tittle-tattle and at the same time

discouraging the restless Brousse from flying off to commit a nuisance somewhere else, a plan had been devised to keep the fidget literally in her place. Grondin had gone foraging and brought in an enormous quantity of grubs, small worms, seeds and bird-bait of all kinds, with his own speciality of crushed acorns. The stock seemed more than any magpie could master, and Hurlaud was depending on the calculation that Brousse's notorious greed would conquer the restlessness of her curiosity and her morbid quest for mischief.

Brousse had been happily excluded. Plantagenet, alas, was also absent. It had not been possible to warn him. He knew that the meeting would take place some time that afternoon, but the hour had been uncertain. Grondin was disappointed, but there was consolation that the time was not known to anyone around La Tranchée. For the farm was in ferment all through that day, and observations from the forest had led to the conclusion that not even the tiniest messenger would have been able to get through. Puissard the sparrow-hawk had gallantly volunteered, but Hurlaud had considered the risk too great and had declined the offer. 'Don't fret about this,' Hurlaud had told Grondin. 'If it was absolutely imperative, I would get somehow to Plantagenet myself. It is not of that urgency. You will have time to brief him of the decisions of the Council before we start the retreat.'

The meeting therefore began. Uhlan formally opened it, speaking at first in a voice that was troubled and quavering: 'My friends, on the advice of Messire Hurlaud des Grands Bois I have decided to call an extraordinary meeting of the Grand Council of the Forest here. I thank you for your attendance. At the present time grave dangers menace our community. You have all been informed of these. It would be useless to go into further detail here.'

He sighed, then continued in a more confident voice:

'We have to organize our temporary flight from these parts. Contacts have been made with Les Fosses, with Vauballiers, with Paitout, all in the forest of Chizé where we have family or friends.'

A murmur arose among the audience. At last they were going to know the details of their retreat.

'Our reception is, I trust, provided for. I have asked our friends that we should be met and given a temporary escort during our initiation. We shall receive there all the help, shelter and protection that can be desired. Bafrin set out this morning with a message for Rohart the suzerain boar, who should be very well known to Grondin since he is one of his ancestors. Bafrin should be back before the end of this meeting and will give us the final details of what has been organized on our behalf.

'Hurlaud, whom you see on my right, has organized a strategic retreat and will shortly disclose the planning, the order of march, and the route to be followed. But first I ask every one present to hold as an absolute secret the arrangements which are to be revealed. The lives of all of us depend on it. I call on Hurlaud to speak. May God protect us, friends.'

When the whispering was stilled Hurlaud got up. He paced back and forth for a little time, taking the gauge of the meeting with his piercing eye. Silence fell. Then he spoke with absolute steadiness:

'The rendezvous for all who wish to join our column is this very spot in Les Combles. The time is five o'clock tomorrow morning, and not seven. Every one must be there. We shall not wait for anyone. We cannot.'

Dame Albaine, who was not put off from voicing her objections immediately, however steady the declamation she was interrupting, asked a question:

'But why not set off earlier?'

'Because, Madame, the noise made by our assembly and

departure, and the scent we shall release all together, will alert the dogs of the farm enclosures on the edge of the forest. It will be black night. If, for example, we decide to set out at midnight, or three in the morning, we must seriously disturb the silence of the night, we cannot help it. The enemy will be engaged in a continuous night-long armed watch. Dogs and men off duty will sleep with only half an eye. It is my considered conclusion that if we give them that sort of warning we shall come up against them within a quarter of an hour after leaving the forest. Our most difficult task is the stretch after the forest, to reach the river and cross the plain without opposition. Once we have alerted the enemy they will be out there, organized with torches and firebrands, and it will be a massacre. Those who are best acquainted with the route to be followed are Grondin – your husband, Dame Albaine – Baclin, your cousin Plantagenet who happily will be with us, and myself. What would happen if by chance one of us went astray in the dark, or if the young panicked and fled across the plain? To this day none of them has yet seen a live flame. Have you thought of that, Dame Albaine?'

Dame Albaine shivered and kept quiet. She was a creature who listened only to her heart, and in her heart there was only one desire: to put as great a distance as possible, and as quickly as possible, between her youngsters and those unknown men outside the forest who were now being referred to as The Enemy.

Hurlaud was continuing his address. 'I pay a direct tribute here when I tell you that the timing and the routing of our exodus owes everything to one noble soul. That we have been warned of what is being hatched is the work of Plantagenet, Grondin's cousin. And it is Plantagenet's knowledge of the forest and of the habits and thinking and even last-minute changes in plan of the enemy that we shall rely on most heavily tomorrow. Plantagenet will join us in time to lead the retreat. Unfortunately we have not been able to contact him so that he could attend this Council. However, Grondin has been able to use this morning to get confirmation of the statements of his cousin and to prove positively that Brousse the magpie has deliberately sought to harm us. We know now for certain that it is of life-and-death importance to fix the departure time for five o'clock, two hours before the assembly of the battue intended to encircle and destroy us. If we had listened to Brousse we should have set off at seven o'clock, and inevitably we should have come face to face with the first lines of the beaters in the plain, completely without cover. I propose to settle accounts with this scum of a magpie later. For the moment, please pay attention to the battle order of the retreat.'

There was a stir as the audience shifted stance. Everyone was well aware that Brousse had a pretty shabby character but none imagined that the magpie could contemplate treachery of such a scale.

Hurlaud raised his voice: 'At the head, Plantagenet. A few paces to his rear, Baclin, my cousin Melheu and the numerous wolves allied with them who will furnish the advance guard. Some paces behind, you, Dame Albaine, with your family and all nursing mothers, non-combatant sows, child-minders and marcassins below fighting age among the boar herds. Covering you on either side will be a half-company of combatant boars selected by Bursiat. But Bursiat will have special duties. I myself will normally be located with Grondin on the forward left flank. But we shall be roving, for part of our responsibility is to whip in the rear and keep ranks well closed up. Behind the youngsters and the sick, lame and lazy in the boar contingent there will march in tight column Dame Pernale in general supervision of the cubs and non-combatants among the wolves, and Dame Tibelle, similarly organizing the foxes, and I should like Dame Pernisse, if she would be so good – I have not had time to make a personal request – to take charge of the disposition of our other shorter-legged friends who will accompany us, in accordance with suggestions she can obtain after this meeting from Mesdames Pernale and Tibelle.' Here Hurlaud smiled a vast smile which he contrived to make more unctuous than wolfish, then went on in a more business-like manner:

'Flandrin and his brother bears will be responsible for defence on the rear flanks.

'I emphasize one point. Plantagenet is the one you must follow. Don't be distracted by Baclin and Melheu and the other wolves. They are there to force a passage if any such necessity arises. They will meet the men and the dogs head on and will engage them as long as possible.

'If anything happens to Plantagenet, Grondin will take his place as leader and then you must follow Grondin.'

'But,' objected Flandrin the bear, 'if it comes to a fight, the group forming the advance guard won't carry much weight. Why not put some of us bears at the head? There are plenty of us.'

'Because your backsides are stuffed with lead,' said Hurlaud with a thin smile. 'You've got the weight all right, but not the speed. Make a good job of escorting the youngsters and getting them as fast as possible to the underwood at Les Fosses; that's all I ask of you. Don't worry about anything else if everything goes according to plan. If there's a hitch up at our end you'll be seeing plenty of action. If all the wolves go down in the fight it will be up to the bears to take over a direct attack and force a passage. You'll have enough on your plate.

'You will be slow,' said Hurlaud grimly, 'but you will deploy far more power than we could. If you do have to take over, remember that once we have crossed the plain and are into the forest on the other side, it will be up to you to supervise defence for our people until you make contact with our fighting friends.

'The tail of the column will be brought up by a rearguard consisting of all the combatant boars not previously detailed by Bursiat, but Bursiat himself and his family have been allocated special duties. Their job is to weave around the column, whipping in stragglers and keeping a particular look-out for any group of youngsters who may go astray after an incident: and to be precise about what I mean by "after an incident" I refer to the possibility of our column being put into complete disorder after a charge by the enemy.'

Fulgent had a question: 'Foxes? I'm not absolutely clear about our job.'

'You will hold the right flank with Fléton and his forces, but keep an eye on Grondin and myself.'

Hurlaud paused to lap a few mouthfuls of water from a nearby puddle, and then gave the assembly his final exhortation:

'As soon as we have reached the far forests at Les Fosses my cousins will be there to welcome us. We shall be under their escort from then on. If we are attacked in the undergrowth outside, I think reinforcements from Chizé should be able to come up in main strength. One last reminder. Plantagenet is the one to follow. If he goes down, follow Grondin. Cancel, repeat, cancel, the seven o'clock start. March at five. And keep your traps shut.'

At that moment Bafrin the falcon flew in, completely out of breath, and settled near Hurlaud. In a few words the lord of the wolves outlined the plan to which they were committed. Bafrin took a minute to get his breath back, and reported: 'All is prepared in Chizé from Les Fosses to Vaubaliers. Our forage is assured.' Being no conversationalist and having nothing further to report that seemed relevant, Bafrin abruptly stopped speaking and eased his muscles with a long stretch. The meeting broke up. In little groups every one went back to his den or to a nearby lair to which he had been invited as a guest.

Uhlan the Wise stayed a few minutes more with Grondin, Hurlaud and Bafrin. Everything seemed to have been organized with competence. 'I shall be able to be of use to you during the day,' said Bafrin. 'Puissard and I will watch out over the plain and warn you of any danger.'

'Good,' agreed Uhlan approvingly. 'My best move will be to go back to my tree. From there I'll be able to see without being seen. When the danger seems less acute, say in two or three days, I'll take a turn to Vauballiers and let you know the lie of the land. I anticipate that after some time you will be able to come back to your dens, but in small groups, of course, and only at night. I'll keep a weather eye open and prime you with the facts.' And with some effort Uhlan soared and flew off towards La Pierre Levée.

Night began to close down on the forest. The mist seemed to drift in from the gloomy underwood and took over the glade of Les Combles. Grondin was taking leave of Hurlaud before lumbering off home when he jumped with sudden recollection and said: 'Hurlaud, the hedge-rat! We've got to see what happened to Lupiot. Pray to God that our apprentice sorcerer had enough charm, or knew enough charms, to keep that double-faced busybody talking in one place without thrusting her long nose into another.'

'Devil take me,' said Hurlaud. 'I had almost forgotten. Let's be going. But, no noise, in case that snake-in-the-grass is still performing.'

The unlucky Lupiot was exhausted. For the whole of the duration of the Council he had kept Dame Brousse in conversation and shared her gargantuan meal. The magpie's belly was distended far beyond fashionable plumpness. She was going into dreamy ecstasies on the wonderful life-style, the incredible hospitality, of Lupiot. 'You have *crammed* me, Lupiot, pressed down and flowing over. Never in my life have I been entertained so royally. What a banquet, my dear! By Jove, but you do things well. I shall never be able to tell you how much I appreciate your style. You are a lord in these parts, a veritable lord, Messire Lupiot.' In the sheer abandon of pleasure the magpie rolled in the grass as was her habit. Lupiot thought dully of a few courtly things to say back, but knew that he had said everything in his small repertoire. The only emotion he could now recognize in his heart was a boiling rage against that liar Grondin, who had assured him that entertaining Brousse would take a far shorter time than it actually had. While Brousse rolled in the grass voluptuously as if the movement was part of the menu in a Roman orgy Lupiot was casting needling looks of anguish into the thicket in the desperate hope of seeing the piratical muzzle of that confidence trickster Grondin appear at last. What a fine show Grondin had put up. And what a dance he had led him. Grondin had brought in with flamboyant ceremony an enormous stock of provisions. Lupiot had hoped that he would be able to keep at least a proportion for himself, and indeed that had been part of the bargain. But Dame Brousse had done much more than honour to what had been sumptuously offered her. The poor hedge-rat suddenly realized that the succulent supplies ferried in by Grondin might actually not last out the entertainment. The party went on. Time seemed not to move, yet the magpie's beak continually moved, grub going in and gabble coming out. By twilight, between guzzling and nattering, not a crumb of food remained.

'Hell and Hecate grill Grondin for ever and ever amen,' groaned Lupiot with the exquisite skill born of desperation that enabled him to say the whole curse without Brousse seeing his lips move. 'Hell and Hecate grill Grondin who has defalcated diddled and done me.' There was a fixed smile on Lupiot's face but his eyes were ceaselessly searching behind Brousse's head. Then suddenly he heard a light crackle and saw an enormous snout come gently through the bush – but not very far.

'Not a moment too soon!' Lupiot shouted, almost beside himself.

'It will never be too soon to repeat such a deliriously delightful banquet,' said Brousse, determined not to let Lupiot interrupt her monologue at this stage, and she continued her interminable declaration of rapture. Lupiot decided that, since the idiot smile was doing nothing but encourage the endless flow of words, he had better simulate sleep. When gentle snores had no effect he decided to have a nightmare. The prospect of having to nurse her host through convulsions decided Brousse to take her leave, and with a curt, 'See you soon, look after yourself,' to the apparently unconscious Lupiot she flew away, even more heavily than the aged Uhlan.

Hardly had she cleared the nearest cluster of trees than Grondin burst out, followed by Hurlaud. 'Congratulations, Lupiot,' said Grondin expansively. 'You have successfully combined with brute greed to convert Dame Brousse from her fidgety addiction to travelling.'

'What time do you think it is?' said the hedge-rat, spitting with rage. 'You double-faced twicer, Grondin, I made a bad bargain with you. Hell and Hecate grill you, Grondin, for you have defalcated diddled and done me.' And this time the hedge-rat used his lips and teeth. Hurlaud keeled over with laughter, which put the lid on Lupiot's indignation. Grondin was just in time to hold him by one paw before he disappeared down his tiny burrow.

Hurlaud and Grondin saw themselves doomed to spend a considerable time soothing the anger of the diminutive rat, and the emotional torture which followed appalled Hurlaud so much that he suddenly disappeared and left Grondin to face the fury of the rodent. Grondin could not get a word in. He had never imagined that such energy could be emitted from such a small body. 'For once and for all, SHUT UP, LUPIOT!' Grondin roared at one stage, and for the few seconds during which the hedge-rat felt the beginnings of fear there was silence – until anger and injured pride took over again, and the harsh voice began to grate even more loudly. In exhaustion Grondin lay down and waited patiently for everything to pass, his muzzle between his trotters, his eyes fixed on vacancy. Gradually he began to study with genuine interest this small beast sitting upright on his invisible behind to raise himself sufficiently to extend a menacing paw towards the snout of a boar who was practically grovelling in the dust, certainly blowing up clouds of it every time he breathed. The teeth of the hedge-rat, Grondin decided, were aesthetically and eugenically too long. They impeded his articulation. His imperfect articulation congested his thought. His congested thought entangled his arguments, his faltering logic paralysed his jaws, disarranged the interplay of his over-long teeth, and caused him to peter out into silence. Only his little black eyes fixed on Grondin spoke eloquently of his bitterness. Realizing his impotence, Lupiot suddenly subsided, crossed his paws, and waited for a response. At this moment Hurlaud reappeared, carrying in his jaws a large leaf in which were wrapped some acorns, chestnuts, medlars and hazels. Keeping his face as straight as he could, Hurlaud laid the offering at Lupiot's feet. The gift was acknowledged by a faint inclination of the head and an incredibly swift acrobatic sweep of the back paws which sent the lot out of sight down the hole in a trice. Lupiot was secretly singing a rhapsody at having acquired enough fodder to last the winter. But all that came out of his mouth was a dirge about the ordeal he had had to undergo with Brousse at the suggestion of

Grondin and Hurlaud. The two animals made suitable apologies and retired as quickly as possible, with a final warning from Hurlaud: 'Dig yourself in well, Lupiot, and don't risk that dappled muzzle outside this hole for at least three days. The enemy have ferrets as well as dogs. Uhlan will come by to see you and tell you how things are going.'

Lupiot suddenly disappeared as if he had drawn a trap door over his head. '*Parturiunt montes,*' observed Hurlaud reflectively, '*nascitur ridiculus mus.*'

'I beg your pardon?' asked Grondin.

'It's Latin,' Hurlaud explained. 'I believe you were a classicist, but we've adopted the revised pronunciation since you were a stripling. Anyway, I don't think I shall translate it just now. I might give you a very rude version.'

14
The Break-Out

At La Tranchée what had previously been simple confusion had grown into intensified uproar. Monsieur Jehan, the master of the horse at the Château de Crespin, had suddenly arrived with three subordinate horsemen. Ostensibly he came to ascertain the number of people at the farm who could be put on the battle roll of Messire de Frébois, and to acquaint Brémand of the exact hour of assembly at the castle. The actual purpose of his visit was more precise. Brémand was a sensitive man. He was well used to the fact that after riding in the country or hunting in the forest Messire de Frébois and his friends were happy to stop at La Tranchée to refresh their bodies and restore their spirits. To this end Jehan had brought a supply of provisions and some packs of plate, and Brémand was by no means offended. He knew Messire de Frébois, he appreciated the care he gave to every detail of hospitality, and he welcomed the attitude of his lord who was determined not to unload on his farmers entertainment expenses for which they were not responsible. 'But,' protested Brémand to Jehan – it must be admitted, largely as a matter of form – 'I presume I may take it that Messire will at the least not despise a draught or two of my own wine.'

'That is agreed,' said Jehan, remembering with an inward smile Messire de Frébois's words on that very matter:

'Brémand is a proud man. He will accept victuals without protest, but will never hear a word about wine. Don't annoy him on this subject, he's very touchy. Tell him we'll be proud to do honour to his casks.' Jehan thought he could expand on that for the sake of a diplomatic inflation of Brémand's pride, and he told the farmer: 'As far as wine is concerned – these are Messire de Frébois's very words – he said, "Leave that to Brémand. I don't know anyone who could do better."'

Brémand, as anticipated, puffed himself up with the flattery and invited Jehan to taste his famous rosé. They followed this with a tour of the estate.

Everything was shining like new, as clean as could be wished. Jehan sincerely complimented Maister Brémand. Then he came to the pig-sty in the second courtyard. He said with surprise: 'Is that your pig, Brémand? Great God, that animal is thin! Is he ill?'

'Ah, Monsieur Jehan, if you only knew the work I have done to try to give that beast a better figure! I can only consider it as a cross that I have to bear. This Plantagenet, for that is his name, regularly refuses any food which is not given him from the hands of my daughter. And even when he takes it from her, he hardly touches a thing. Many a time I have had a good mind to get rid of him, for I have done my sums and it is plain that this animal yields no profit. But . . .' and Brémand hesitated in embarrassment for a moment, scratched his head, and then went on: 'You must understand that he was given to me by my brother. I can't give him away. And Adèle has fallen for the wretch. She thinks he is very intelligent.'

'Intelligent!' said Jehan. 'Pull the other one.'

'Oh yes,' said Brémand. 'Would you believe that she has taught him all sorts of tricks. He can open and shut doors. He cleans up the courtyard like a farm hand . . . . Believe me, he's no ordinary pig. I'll even admit,' said Brémand taking Jehan confidentially by the arm, 'that the grown-ups here are quite attached to this beast. I know damn well it's stupid, but when he isn't here we miss him.'

'This is sensational,' said Jehan. 'You should put on a circus for your guests. With this pig as a star, what a success you would score!'

The two men laughed and continued their stroll.

Plantagenet had heard everything, though he had been pretending to be fast asleep. 'Funny fellow!' he snorted with disgust at the retreating outline of the groom. Then he went over the conversation again in his mind and began to enjoy a certain satisfaction from it. Brémand seemed to have no intention of slaughtering him, and that was good news indeed. But Brémand had also implied that he was not despised, he was appreciated, even missed in his absence. That was gratifying in the extreme. He thought glumly that he might even persuade himself to be cheerful if he had not already enrolled for the most dangerous mission in his life. His life? – how long would that last? The most he could promise himself was that he would die happy, for the love of Adèle, or at the literal least 'because the grown-ups here are quite attached to this beast'.

Plantagenet felt sick in his stomach. What was happening at Les Combles? No messenger had arrived from Hurlaud or Grondin. No one had been able to get through to La Tranchée, and for the same reason it would be very difficult for Plantagenet to get out of La Tranchée without sounding an alarm. It was imperative that he should leave the farm soon, before the gates were shut, at the very latest by nine o'clock, and then he would have to speed like an arrow to Les Combles. Night was no trouble to him. He knew the way perfectly. What would be serious would be if anyone saw him leave and raised a hue and cry on the farm which might end in the organization of a hunt for him, led by Hargneu. It was a possibility that troubled him deeply. He saw vividly in his imagination the hunt, the chase, his pursuers finally catching up on him near Les Combles, just when Grondin, Dame Albaine and the youngsters were preparing for their departure. A terrible confrontation! Made all the worse because Hargneu would immediately notice the difference in size between Grondin and the 'boar' called Grondin who had not only humiliated him but earned him a thrashing that very afternoon. What a situation! Plantagenet buried himself in his straw, feeling already in his hams the remorseless grip of Hargneu's jaws.

He came out of his litter determined to reassure himself and have a good laugh at his fears. Instead, he began to worry about a new sequence of disaster. He had to stay quiet, waiting until the last moment to get away. But the risk was that the gates would be shut and he would not be able to get out at all. What would happen to the expedition he was supposed to lead? His friends would all be waiting for him to take the head. Time would be lost while they waited. Eventually, no doubt, Grondin would take over the post of leader. But what then if by bad luck they came across the men-at-arms? What carnage! Frightful scenes passed before his eyes. He saw his dear cousin pierced through and through with lance thrusts. He saw the hounds unleashed on the column of youngsters and their minders, retreating in disarray, no longer knowing which saint to vow to or what direction to take, a column which had no one to guide them and scattered diffusely for easy slaughter. Poor Albaine! Poor marcassins! Yes, even poor Pielet! Little by little Plantagenet disappeared, by the very vibrations of his trembling fear, down into his litter again. One thing Brousse had said was certainly right. What a responsibility he had taken on. But, from the moment it was known that he had failed, what a reputation the survivors would give him! He would no longer dare to put his head outside La Tranchée. Any fine day when he risked taking a turn outside the walls

he would be sure to be met by Hurlaud and his pack, or
Baclin and his, or probably both! He saw himself dragged by
the ears, trotters, tail – anything handy to that savage crew –
to the place of judgment. There would be a period of
impassioned denunciation. Then he would be put to death.
The thought of being eaten alive by this army of avenging
wolves caused such a tremor in his limbs that, even although
he was no longer visible, the whole heap of his bed began to
shake.

Rupert, who was passing by, was very surprised to see the
straw pulsating in such plunging jerks. He stopped to
investigate, probed with his muzzle, and found a pink
object, which happened to be one of Plantagenet's hind
trotters. Plantagenet, who was at the climax of despair in the
waking nightmare he was going through, suddenly felt a
cold nose touch his thigh. He gave a terrible howl, braced
his strength, shot like a cross-bolt, and buried his head in
the near wall. Half stunned, but raving even more than
aching, he shrieked as he writhed: 'Help! Let me go! It's
not true! I'm not a traitor!'

'Hey, Plantagenet, my old friend,' said Rupert very
concerned, 'what's the matter with you? Are you ill?'

Plantagenet came back into this world. His first action
was to make a close examination of the wall against which
he had just launched his head. 'Oh my God, I'm dead!' he
concluded. Rupert, now very distracted, tried to calm his
friend as best he could, and repeatedly asked what had so
upset him. Plantagenet could not utter a sound, but merely
squinted uglily at the enormous bump which was growing
on his forehead. After some time he consented to sit down
and sip some drops of fresh water. He thanked Rupert for
his affectionate concern.

'But tell me, Plantagenet, what has put you in such a state?'

Plantagenet paused. 'I . . . I've . . . had a very bad dream.
I . . . I saw myself eaten alive by Hargneu.'

Plantagenet secretly congratulated himself on having thought of this lie. He had not quite lost his wits and he could not afford indiscreet confidences at that time. Rupert smiled indulgently and comforted the pig as best he could. Then he said maliciously: 'With the drubbing you have given Hargneu so recently he is bound to seek a quarrel with you sooner or later. You will have to invest in this wonderful soot which seems to work better than war-paint. . . .'

'Ah, so you've been told!'

'No, I saw it all for myself. Don't worry. I shan't say a word in the wrong places. But I wish I had known before what a cunning practical joker you are.'

Plantagenet felt his self-esteem rising, which helped his general recovery. He got up, with some difficulty, and then asked Rupert point blank: 'Are you taking part in to-morrow's carnival?'

'Carnival?' said Rupert. 'Your information on that point is not very reliable.' He lowered his voice. 'What is being planned is a veritable war of extermination against the natural predators of the forest.' He sighed. 'I am going, yes, but much against my will, believe me.'

Plantagenet put on a show of knowing nothing of what was being prepared, or at least of having scraps of inconsequential information. This encouraged Rupert to pass on other confidences of what was being whispered on the farm, but none of them added to the information which the forest already had. The rendezvous was fixed at the castle at five o'clock and the assembly of the separate sections of the battue in the precise points allocated to them was to be at seven. Rupert knew nothing more. Plantagenet realized that in all that armed camp only he knew that the departure of the animals was to be at five o'clock from Les Combles, and he realized that he must keep his secret to the end, but above all, at whatever cost, get out of La Tranchée without being observed. In no way was this to be an easy matter.

'I feel a little breath of fresh air would do me good,' he suggested.

Rupert was delighted that he seemed more himself again. 'Go on, friend, take a breather,' he said jovially. 'Far better to wake yourself up with an invigorating breeze than start on any more of these dreams that send you diving into stone walls.'

'Stone walls! Little does he know!' Plantagenet told himself with a touch of cheerful melodrama as he went outside and made a complete circuit of the farmstead boundary to see if he could come across any prospective exit other than the front porch. At one point he heard voices and discreetly faded behind an out-house. Maister Brémand and the master of horse Jehan were also having a promenade. They had stopped in front of Hargneu's kennel. The dog, restrained on a tight lead, was looking very sorry for himself.

'Is that one of your mastiffs, Brémand? What has happened to him? He seems pretty cowed.'

'I've just had to settle an account with that brute. I took him for an honest obedient animal but he's not played fair with me.' Brémand recounted the incident of the sausage. 'No matter, he'll get his liberty in time for the battue tomorrow. He may be a bit vague about meum and tuum but he's got plenty of spirit. He'll be very useful to us, he's a courageous brute and no wolf will scare him.'

Out of sight, Plantagenet made a face at the men. If Brémand thought that Hurlaud and Baclin and their pack were going to stay and wait for that mob to hustle them out they had another think coming. Plantagenet continued his tour of the outside wall. But he could find no crack or cranny that gave him any hope of getting through it. The one possibility he found was a balk of timber in a peculiar position near the well. One end of this beam was sunk into the ground. The other end rested on the top of the wall. The slope was very steep, but it might be possible with a good run to scramble up it and finish up astride the top of the wall. How exactly one got over and down the other side had better be left to the future. It was a stroke of luck to come across this beam, which Maister Brémand had planted as the buttress of a shelter he intended to build in order to hang up neatly all the tubs and buckets which now lay higgledy-piggledy near the well.

Plantagenet prospected the site, trying to look casual but unable to resist a savage glare at the tub still full of water in which Edmond had dunked him not so long ago. Then, very cautiously, he began to test whether he could climb the beam. He was unaware that at this moment Brémand and Jehan had suddenly interrupted their adieux to gaze open-mouthed at the spectacle of a pig balancing on a sloping balk of timber. Things were not going too well. After a few hesitant steps Plantagenet slipped. But he recovered himself rather neatly, let himself fall on his belly on to the beam, and glided gracefully to the ground. He tried again. This time he managed to get higher up the timber, curving his back in an effort to keep steady as the steepness of the slope affected him. Then, suddenly, he was overcome by a sensation he had never felt before. He was giddy. The ground seemed to recede at an unimaginable speed, and yet at the same time it was drawing him towards it like a witch casting a spell. His eyes glazed. He saw two beams, then three beams, and he put his front trotter on the middle one. But it wasn't there. He had no support at all, and with a shriek of fear he felt himself snatched into the void and, a second later, suffocating in a tub of icy water. Not far away, two great shouts of laughter sent the doves wheeling from their cote. Maister Brémand and Monsieur Jehan were in convulsions. 'What a clown you have, Brémand. You must never never send him to the kitchen. Set him up in show business and he will give you a one-man cabaret.'

'Isn't that what I was just saying? But this is the first time he has done this particular trick. He has put on a preview just for you, Monsieur Jehan.'

Mortified with shame, Plantagenet streaked back to his bed and dived in. It took him some time to get warm and dry again, longer to regain his composure. Desperately he pulled himself together and decided to make a final dash out of the farm. He went to the main gate. But bad luck was dogging him. After letting his guest out, Maister Brémand had himself carefully closed the heavy iron-bound doors. Plantagenet made one more circuit of the walls but found no other way out. He resigned himself to wait past nightfall and make a last effort to clamber up the beam.

The farmstead was quiet, as though exhausted by the unusual excitement which had gripped it all through the afternoon. Before the gates were shut, Henriot, Jacquet and Faucheux, Brémand's nearest neighbours, had arrived at La Tranchée. It had been agreed that the forces of the four farms would meet at La Tranchée early next morning and form a combined troop to make their way to the castle. A single hunting pack would be formed, and the rendezvous at Brémand's was to be at half-past three. Consequently at an early hour in the night the farm in the lee of the forest was plunged in torpor as the inhabitants rested before the rigours of the morrow.

Plantagenet emerged, seeking to make himself as small as possible. Nothing excited his suspicion. A fine penetrating rain, blowing in strongly from dead north, made him shiver for a moment. He snorted, and quickly stilled the sound. Walking in little steps, his heart beating, beating, beating, he made his way towards the balk of timber. He concentrated for a long time, calculating his chances. Then with a low, hoarse cry, his ears forward and his tail back like a spike, he took off, charged the beam, went straight up it without even seeing it, reached the wall with a single burst and lay spread-eagled across it. He see-sawed to the other side, plummeted into black space, and succumbed to the disaster which seemed exclusively reserved for him in the book of Fate. He was head under in the muddy water of the moat.

Chilled, numbed and half-suffocated, he struggled to the edge and clambered out of the mire amid an explosion of profanity which Adèle could not even have spelt. He lifted his nose to the wind and rushed hell for leather into the forest along the track to Les Combles.

Not a soul at La Tranchée was aware that he had gone. Hargneu, still nominally a guard dog but confined to kennels by the strangling leash, had decided that as an unacknowledged political prisoner he would renounce all formal obligations, and had relaxed in sulky sleep. If Fate seemed biased against Plantagenet in an insistence on excessive baptism, an inscrutable natural justice had extended compensation through the outcome of the Affair of the Purloined Sausage.

An hour later, frothing at the mouth and exuding a whitish mist which effectively doubled his small size, Plantagenet shot into the clearing at Les Combles. Grondin was awake. He had insisted that his family should rest before the long march, but he could not sleep himself. He had much on his mind, the calculation of chances and the personal dispositions which every father of a family has to consider at a time of crisis. He had talked with Dame Albaine, making arrangements to cover every foreseeable mischance, and he knew at the end of it that they were neither of them easy in their minds. Dame Albaine had tried to persuade him to let her stay up with him, but it had been a relief to him to send her to bed and stop the continual exchange of worried glances. Grondin, the proud and surly boar who secretly enjoyed his reputation as the king curmudgeon, was awake and alone and continuously sighing as he watched Dame Albaine and their youngsters sleeping into the dawn. Plantagenet's arrival snatched him from his gloomy thoughts.

'Ah, there you are, old friend. Come in, cousin, come in and rest. I was thinking you could hardly be much longer.' He cleared his throat with a rasp. 'Everything is organized. Hurlaud is taking pretty big risks, but in my view there is no alternative. I'll tell you everything, but for goodness sake rest. You're wet through with sweat. Don't stay in that corner, there's a draught and you'll catch your death. Come over here, where at least I can keep you in my sights.'

Grondin brought Plantagenet up to date with all the details of the operation. Plantagenet listened, in some exhaustion, half asleep and half awake. But from the concise orders being detailed by his cousin he kept one essential instruction firmly in the front of his mind: keep ahead at all costs; make straight for Les Fosses without diversion; do not falter on account of any ambush that is threatened.

'Everyone will be forming up by half-past four,' said Grondin. 'We must start by five at the latest. We must be as far as possible on our way before things warm up.'

With a last sigh, Grondin cast a long look at his four youngsters. By instinct Plantagenet followed the look, then suddenly sat on his tail. The memory of Pielet's teeth was still lively in his mind.

15

The Battue

Muffled in a goatskin cloak, Maister Henriot slept until the last moment, waiting for Jacquet and Faucheux to get up before him. The women of La Tranchée were already up, and were busy around the ovens, for Messire de Frébois had strictly ordered that everyone should take a substantial meal before going into action. The dogs wandered around in the dark courtyard, happy to be taking part in something out of the ordinary and infecting each other with excitement. Hargneu had been released from the punishment cell, and circulated among the home-farm dogs and the visitors – whom he knew well from other mass excursions – re-establishing his prestige as leader of the pack as skilfully as he could. Before long every dog in the yard was glowing with the gossip that this was really to be *Der Tag*, the day when all the motley farm dogs in the county would come into their own and win a famous victory against the savage forest marauders – and all would be done without the specialized hunting hounds of the Messires, who would be exposed to ridicule in Poitou and eventually become the laughing-stock of Aquitaine, all because of the ineffably brilliant ambush devised by Hargneu the Great, Canine Lord of La Tranchée, eternally mindful of his feudal loyalty to his suzerain Brémand, in spite of a false accusation by his master that he had been involved in a sordid theft.

Brousse's plan had been that at seven that morning Plantagenet should lead the column of forest animals in retreat, at a time when the extended hollow square had already formed àll round them. The route Plantagenet was taking to Chizé led to that sector of the square where the forces of Messire de Frébois were to be advancing in line abreast. Since, as well as the contingent from La Tranchée, there were five other companies among the forces immediately commanded by Messire de Frébois, there was very strong pressure on the dogs from La Tranchée to spot the approaching animals first, if they were to win the race for glory. Since the La Tranchée curs were the only pack to have an advance warning, and their enemies were walking head on into an ambush down a known path, the requirement was merely for the compulsive heroes to monopolize the track from Les Combles to Chizé and have distant scouts flung far forward.

Hargneu did not outline this easy conquest in its original crudity, but decorated it with combatant details and invented a few fantasy-risks to keep the adrenalin flowing before he tried his eloquence on a final peroration:

'I see you stand like greyhounds in the slips, straining upon the start,' he howled. 'The game's afoot. And yet you have the greater glory because you are *not* greyhounds, bloodhounds, otterhounds, *not* the cosseted chiefs of the chase, *not* the effete, the élite, the in-bred, the over-lavished so-called aristocracy of the hunting-field, daintily sired and dammed to fit a family tree for pedantic lordlings who see perfection only in a pedigree. We are the common dogs of the country, lustily sired by natural affection. We have no family trees of parchment. The only trees we recognize are of wood, and we know what to do against them. We are the bastards, the mongrels, the nameless, the little-loved, of whom they speak with such scorn up at the Castle. Yet it is we who will carve out the glory in the battle ahead of us.

Naturally our success will redound to our masters. But that is no disadvantage to us. From now on they will show us the deference we deserve.' He cast a bitter look at Rupert, the only dog of any breeding in the yard, who stood apart, impassively watching the climax of the performance. 'Therefore be firm, dear friends and fellow bastards. Close your ranks, and not one whimper until I sound. Keep your eyes open, your noses peeled, and your faith in your leader untainted. In a short time we shall be in action. I tell you now that at a determined point between here and Donkey Bottom a battle will be joined, a victory will be won, that will shower crowns of laurel on us, my friends, the sons of the soil, the common dogs of the country.'

A trumpet sounded. 'Fall in everyone!' shouted a man on horseback. There was a hubbub of barking, which Hargneu quickly stilled. Amid the jingle of harness and the clattering of spears and maces, the expedition formed up under the eyes of the ladies and filed through the main gate. Riding together at the head were Brémand, Henriot, Jacquet and Faucheux. Behind them rode the chosen contingent of the men from the four fiefs, twenty-five in all, a little embarrassed in their new hunting habits and not too obviously at ease on their horses. Around them scrambled all the dogs, Hargneu racing importantly to front and rear of the cohort, ferreting in the bushes, gradually yielding to the excitement of the occasion yet using his authority to keep an effective discipline among the dogs – excepting Rupert, who followed the party showing some signs of disdain, and very ostentatiously in the rear.

The night was cold, but clear enough. The rain had stopped and occasionally a ray of moonlight pierced the sky, pointing silver fingers into the mysterious shadows of the great forest. The way was winding, and the leading dogs wove between pot-holes and quagmires which had been partly caused and wholly aggravated by the heavy wheels of

the clumsy carts which used the track. The party had set off
in good time and kept up a reasonable speed. Yet an
atmosphere of anxiety seemed gradually to grow, and im-
perceptibly they began to force the pace.

At this time in the clearing of Les Combles the members
of the forest community were assembling. Hurlaud had been
the first to rouse his family, and as he escorted them to the
glade he poked his nose into Grondin's retreat. 'Good day
to thee, tha bugger,' he saluted Grondin, and added, just as
cordially but with more formality, 'Good day to you,
Plantagenet.'

'Good day to you, Hurlaud,' Plantagenet answered, a little
on edge at seeing Hurlaud so close again. The families
moved off together to the meeting point. There the marcassins and wolf cubs were encouraged to rest under the eyes of
their mothers and, dull with sleep, they flopped down on the
dry grass. Hurlaud, Grondin and Plantagenet went out to
welcome the first arrivals. Baclin soon appeared at the head
of his warrior pack who were to furnish the advance guard.
As the animals passed in front of Plantagenet each gravely
and silently made an inclination of the head, a simple, un-
affected salute from the nobility of the free forest to a
volunteer who had joined them from the dominion of man.
Plantagenet smelt the strong odour of the wolves as they
passed near him. It affected him with an attack of goose
pimples which he was glad he could conceal in the darkness
of the night. What an impressive physique Baclin had, he
told himself, what a resolute appearance they all put up.

Soon the clearing was filled with little groups of animals,
punctuating the silence of the night with short, stifled
exclamations. Hurlaud had briefed them well, no further
orders were necessary. Each understood what was at stake,
and accepted his responsibilities. Yet all were affected by the
one agonizing problem of the youngsters. Could the cubs
keep up with the column headed by this alien leader, who

was possibly unfamiliar with their range of endurance and might not trouble sufficiently about what was happening in the rear? Many mothers took Plantagenet aside to beg him not to force the pace too hard, especially at the start, and to look round from time to time to make sure that the column was keeping up. Plantagenet, tugged between those who wanted to reach Les Fosses as fast as possible and those anxious above all to keep their family together, tried to give assurance to all.

Hurlaud, Baclin and Grondin marshalled the column into the disposition fixed on the previous day. Puissard the sparrowhawk had been commissioned to fly high and spot any youngsters who might go astray. Bafrin the falcon came and took up position near Plantagenet who was now thrilling with the tension of the occasion. 'I shall watch over you, my friend,' said the falcon in a steady voice. 'I shall fly at a good height so that as soon as there is any visibility you can always mark me. Once day breaks, follow me precisely, for I shall be able to indicate the surest and shortest way. If by bad luck you come under attack, I will fly towards you and take on the enemy. If you see me stop short, beat my wings and take another direction, alter course immediately to follow me, for I shall have seen some trap and taken avoiding action.'

With a great whir of feathers Bafrin the Noble flew off.

When everyone was in place, the youngsters locked inside the central group with the rearguard closed up on them, Hurlaud turned to Plantagenet and said in a firm voice:

'Now for it, Monsieur. The fate of our families is in your hands.'

Blushing with tremulous pride at the compliment, Plantagenet took his place at the head of the column and the march began. As he had previously agreed with Hurlaud, Plantagenet plunged forward at a brisk warming-up pace, not too demanding. Then, when he reached Pied du Fût, he lengthened the pace. Behind him everyone was following in

good order. He could hear the physical sounds of marching,
but no animal call, only the strong breathing of a single-
minded company striving to cross the curtain of trees at
Les Fosses before seven o'clock if it could be done.

The column was now in good order. None of the young
animals cried or whimpered. Plantagenet visualized the
terrain ahead, trying to determine at what precise point a
critical meeting between the animals and the hunters might
occur.

On two occasions Hurlaud, weaving from skirmisher to
skirmisher in the advance screen like a despatch courier,
came to the head of the column and marched side by side
with Plantagenet for a few comradely paces. This erstwhile
mortal enemy had lost all menace and spoke to Plantagenet
as equal to equal, even with a touch of the courtliness he
accorded Grondin the boar.

Hurlaud's mind had been active as he checked the disposition of his forces. 'If we are taken on the flank,' he told
Plantagenet, 'for by bad luck we may be caught from the
side, don't let it affect you, but keep up the same pace. If
you follow the line of the river as far as the Souligné bridge
you will come out opposite Les Fosses and you will have a
minimum distance to cover. Follow Bafrin the falcon. We
can't spot him in this light but he is up there marking for us
and it will be after dawn when we really need him.

'If the head of the column is attacked, I want you personally to turn immediately on a right or left incline and make
straight for the enemy. That way, you will cause the greatest
confusion in their ranks. Either Grondin or I will take your
place as leader. I have kept this last decision secret from all
except Grondin, my brother Baclin, Fulgent the fox and
Flandrin the bear. Charge straight at the horses, old man,
and you'll bring off a beautiful shambles when all the
dogs at your heels get tangled with the hooves of the
horses.'

He added with military realism: 'I don't think you will be at very great risk, for that rabble believe you are under their colours. I can't vouch for what the dogs think. But I doubt if the men will let the hounds kill you. You'll take a few bites, but it will be a poor show if the Flying Pig doesn't manage to shake the dogs off.

'Now here we are marching in line with the river. In half an hour we shall have reached the edge of Donkey Bottom. Dawn will still not have broken properly, and with a bit of luck we shall get through.'

He looked Plantagenet steadily in the eye and said: 'If what I fear does happen, I can do nothing for you, Plantagenet, at least until you have got away as far as Les Fosses. From then on you will be in the cover of the brushland and we shall be able to give you protection. With the formation we have had to adopt, we don't dispose of enough force to support you in this diversionary manoeuvre I'm asking of you.'

Plantagenet tossed his head with what he hoped was nonchalance. He was well aware of the risk he was taking, particularly with regard to that fiend Hargneu. He felt a tremor of goose-flesh down his spine. But, oddly enough, he was already less afraid. To be helping such friends without a second thought seemed to him an act of courage of which he had once thought himself incapable. The dice were thrown. 'Plantagenet, forward! You're in the army now. Get weaving, you 'orrible soldier!'

He picked up his step. The column was following, in as tight formation as when they had started.

Little by little the two opposed forces unknowingly approached each other. Both sides became aware that they were coming up to the edge of the open country at Donkey Bottom. The big trees gradually thinned into clusters of thornbush and isolated elms, occasionally lit by a fleeting moonbeam. Soon there were signs of the first clearings. The bare muddy ground showed traces of cart tracks. The air became keener, more biting.

The mastiff Hargneu, alert but believing he had two hours in hand, sniffed the wind, but it brought him nothing. Cantering behind him, muffled in fur-lined cloaks, Maister Brémand and his companions passed occasional comments in guarded tones. Suddenly Hargneu, who had darted out to a clump of trees, felt a strange sensation go through him, a swift wave of uneasiness. Something had happened which had passed as quickly as a flash of lightning, but he had the distinct impression that he had caught an eddy of air charged with that strong smell which wild beasts leave behind them.

He began to grow excited. He turned round. He sniffed again. A little farther on, he had the same sensation. He was still in doubt, and dared not yet give tongue. Then it came again, and this time he was more sure. He checked his bearings. On the right side they were only a few furlongs from the boundary of Donkey Bottom. A fresh draught of the scent tingled in his nose. Now there was no doubt. This was it. But it was not according to plan!

Hargneu stood stock still for a second, buttressed himself and delivered a gigantic bark. Then he raced towards what he had smelt. In an instant the pack of hounds, taken aback but leaving the thinking to Hargneu, rushed after him although many of them had not yet caught the scent. Fired by the excitement of sudden action, they all began to bay as they bounded after Hargneu, leaving the horsemen stupefied with frustration.

'What's happening, Henriot?' Brémand shouted angrily to his companion. 'Those stupid dogs will hold us back. Call back your hounds, man. Hargneu! Hargneu! To heel, you idiot!' Brémand holla'd to his own mastiff.

'They're not stupid, not stupid,' Henriot burst out excitedly. 'Those dogs are on to something. Can't you hear growling, can't you hear branches cracking? Just here on the right? It's the wild beasts! They must have intercepted some fool who gave the game away and they're breaking out to the plain. Well, that's our line of march anyway. Let's cut off their retreat as they come out of the woods. Don't lose time. Mince them to pieces. Let the hounds move them up towards us.'

Henriot dug both heels in his horse and dashed towards the plain. Brémand and the others followed him.

Hurlaud had instinctively sniffed danger well before Hargneu's first cry. He urged Plantagenet: 'Faster, Plantagenet. Increase your pace. Just now I have a certain feeling. . . .' Plantagenet instantly obeyed. He had utter trust in the premonitions of a predator like Hurlaud.

Suddenly Plantagenet heard the voice of Hargneu. He would have known that baying among a thousand. He felt the old familiar shiver prickle his spine. But he had no time to worry about what would happen to him. Already Grondin and Hurlaud had come up alongside him.

Grondin yelled: 'Run fifty paces ahead of us and get ready for action.'

There was a grating cry above them. Bafrin the falcon was signalling danger.

Ears straight up, tail as stiff as it could ever be, his eyes staring and his tongue hanging from one side, Plantagenet shot forward as if impelled by a spring.

The grey of dawn was spreading, smoothing away the darkness. From now on nothing mattered except to get to Les Fosses as fast as possible.

Plantagenet felt pain all through his body. He checked his pace for an instant. He looked round. The column was marching steadily, but at the double now. There was a gap between the advance guard and the main defence group protecting the young cubs. Fifty paces behind Plantagenet, Grondin had a terrifying aspect as he plunged forward, all his hair bristling erect.

Hurlaud had bared his fangs in a sub-conscious tightening
of chap-muscle which gave him a fearful grimace. At his side
his brother Baclin seemed less theatrical but more menacing
as he loped along, his eyes flashing red. The other wolves
ran purposefully behind. And Flandrin, stout Flandrin the
bear, had flatly ignored his orders, had left to his brother
bears the rearguard defence, and had just completed a
superursine effort to heave himself to the head of the party
protecting the youngsters. His frame was straining with the
ordeal, all his eight hundred pounds of muscle and his claws
a foot long.

Plantagenet suddenly felt himself snatched up drunkenly
in the wind. Without being able to remember his movements,
he realized that he had come out on to the plain, which he
could half-see, stretching out in an expanse of pale grey.
Dawn sprouted a little shoot, projecting feeble shafts into
the even moonlight. Lifting his head, Plantagenet could see
the falcon Bafrin a hundred feet above him. It was now
possible to distinguish shapes at three hundred paces distance. Surely those vague figures in the half-light on the left
must be horsemen! Much more surely, that surging wave
coming towards him only two hundred paces away was the
pack of hounds, moving at frightening speed. And Hargneu
was at its head.

Plantagenet quickened his speed. He was now sixty paces
ahead of Grondin. In less than a minute he would be cut off
from the column. Suddenly he heard cries from the left
flank. He distinguished a hollow, panting howl from Baclin
to his brother: 'Look out on your right, Hurlaud! The
enemy is on your right, too.'

With murder in their eyes a fresh pack of hounds broke
cover twenty yards from the wolves. In a perfect manoeuvre
the advance guard re-grouped to receive them. Grondin's
cousins, the boars protecting the other flank of the main
party, had veered in from the right, crossed through the

main group on the march, and ranged themselves with the left-flank fighters.

'Everyone follow Grondin,' shouted Hurlaud to the main party. 'Keep going! Don't get mixed up with the fighters.' Grondin had taken up the leadership of the column in place of Plantagenet. At speed Grondin swung away from the river Guirande, to avoid being cut off by the horsemen, who had already swerved in to intercept them. In a tumult of crashing hooves, pounding pads, breaking branches and sibilant gasps of effort, the panting main party followed Grondin.

Already on the left flank the wolves of the advance guard were in action. In a desperate mêlée twenty wolves were trying to engage and contain over a hundred dogs. The huge Baclin, with all his fangs exposed, rushed on the first mastiff in his path. Well versed in all the tricks of hunting and combat, he made a feint to pass on the right. The dog, eyes starting from its head, stretched its neck to catch Baclin in flight. He exposed his throat. It was what the wolf was waiting for. With a swift movement he suddenly turned and sank all his teeth in the flesh extended to him. He felt the bones crush under the pressure of his jaws, and he loosed hold immediately. One dog had received his account.

'The fattest goes first,' cracked Hurlaud, already hemmed in on all sides. 'Look out, Baclin! Look out to the right!'

Whirling about to face all fronts, lunging with their teeth without getting too deep into the heart of the pack, the wolves had momentarily halted their adversaries. They had achieved their first objective. Now it was urgent to keep the enemy fighting. But the inadequate numbers of the wolves made it almost inevitable that they would go down under the mass of the hounds, who seemed to multiply before their eyes and made a concerted rush on them.

Cerbert, Baclin's brother, attacked by four sturdy mastiffs, went down, bitten all over his body and bleeding from every limb.

Fulmet, a distant cousin of Baclin, who had had a permanent limp since he had succeeded in heaving his right forefoot out of a trap, was at the last extremity. Over-run by the pack, one ear torn off, he still raised his head to meet them. But his loins were badly savaged in an attack from the rear, and he was forced to continue fighting sitting down, his back against a tree.

Baclin himself, in spite of his enormous speed, was surrounded and owed his life to his brother Ferlut, who with one snap finished the mastiff who was launching himself from the rear to catch Baclin's loins. In that moment Ferlut himself was surrounded, and disappeared under the snarling pack.

Hurlaud was face to face with Muquon, the Widow Bigotte's dog. The two animals had had an account to settle ever since the lifting of a certain sheep some days previously. Muquon, who always guarded the flock, had been decisively outplayed in that encounter, and as a consequence he had been severely thrashed by the miserly widow. He had sworn to have the pelt of that damned wolf. He was big, muscular and stocky. There was mastiff blood in his veins. He had more strength than intelligence, but he was feared by all his companions. Once he had almost succeeded in throttling Fulgent the fox, but the bear Flandrin, unexpectedly emerging from the edge of the forest, had forced Muquon to let go his hold. The rogue fox boasted about this for ever after, and used to show off the scar on his throat.

Now Muquon was almost muzzle to muzzle with Hurlaud of the Great Woods, who had deliberately sought him out. This was to be a straight duel, single combat. 'Over to you, Muquon,' said Hurlaud with menace, and he settled himself firmly on his hind legs. All the other combatants instinctively withdrew from the two of them.

But the battle was not abandoned. In the uproar Hurlaud heard the strong voice of his brother: 'They shall not pass! Courage, comrades. Keep them engaged.'

Like an arrow from a bow Hurlaud sprang at Muquon, who made the same feint as Baclin had done earlier, and saw Hurlaud fail to connect. This tough beast knew how to fight, Hurlaud realized, and was skilled in guarding his throat.

Hurlaud used his momentum to swerve as he landed, and he heard Muquon's jaws snap within an inch of his throat. More agile than the mastiff, he had time to turn about before the dog had finished his lunging whirl. Dodging and weaving, his head between his shoulders to offer the smallest possible hold, Hurlaud did a one-two, saw the dog prepare to pounce, wrong-footed him, and as quick as lightning pancaked down as he sliced a deep wound in his enemy's shoulder. At the same time he felt Muquon's jaws close on his skull. The pain was intense, but he had seen others blinded by blood gushing from such yawning wounds, and with enormous vigour he shook himself, and his adversary with him, hard enough almost to break his bones. Muquon, with a shoulder badly damaged, lost his balance and fell to the ground, but he did not let go. He tried desperately to get at the wolf's eyes. Hurlaud ducked his head as his only chance of survival. The dog's teeth tore his spine. But Muquon lost his balance again and Hurlaud, in one neat movement, buried his fangs in the dog's belly. He recognized the howl of Muquon's death-cry. The dog, penetrated in a vital part, little by little relinquished his grip.

At the same moment the wolf felt a fearful pain. Another big mastiff had seized him by the loins and was trying to tear him apart. Wolves cannot turn backwards. A peculiarity of the angle of the ribs and spine makes this movement impossible. They must spring up and jump backwards. If a wolf is held by the hind quarters he cannot free himself.

Hurlaud reared up and gave a howl of distress. Beneath him Muquon shuddered in his last agony, his entrails spouting on to the ground.

Boulet the boar had just arrived to join the fight. He saw at once that Hurlaud was in a desperate state. As quick as a meteor, his tusks at the ready, he charged and literally fell on the dog, who was too intent on the butchery he was effecting on Hurlaud to notice what was happening behind. A second later his unrecognizable body, crushed and disembowelled, was circling in the air to land ten paces away. Boulet now set his great mass of leather to freeing Hurlaud. 'You certainly came at the right time,' said Hurlaud with a wry grimace. 'If it had not been for you, I should have been for it, and so would my brothers.' Indeed, in spite of their courage, the wolves would certainly have gone under. Three of them were already dead, and another ten were in a piteous state. The boars, because of their slow speed, had taken time to come up with the battle. The important thing was that they had arrived, and they made their presence felt in a terrible manner. In the general mêlée Hurlaud could see, to right and left of him, dogs being tossed in all directions. With silent efficiency the boars had thrown themselves on to the last remaining section of the pack, which was going through an exceedingly bad quarter of an hour.

Ten bodies littered the ground. The wounded, as soon as they could stagger to their feet, made off, yelping. The battle was about to turn to the advantage of the forest animals, and more assuredly so with the arrival of another wave of reinforcement. The good bear Flandrin, who had been screening the rear of the column with his family, had posted a certain number of his bears to maintain the rearguard, and brought the rest into the fray. They had followed the tracks of the boars, and now themselves lumbered into battle with mighty blows from their enormous paws tipped with the great tearing claws.

The dogs, more and more uncertain of the outcome of the action, lost their initiative. Suddenly they fled, leaving some twenty of their number already dead or quivering in the last tremors of life. Hurlaud, limping badly, paced the battlefield and summed up the situation.

In the distance, on the right, he could hear men shouting and dogs barking from the other pack, led by Hargneu. They were snapping at the heels of Plantagenet. Hurlaud allowed himself a twisted smile of acknowledgement that his diversionary tactic had worked. The men and the leading pack of hounds were concentrating on hunting down a pig.

As for the main column of animals, the non-combatants with their screen of skirmishers, there was now no doubt that they would be able to get through. The principal objective was attained.

Here, on the battlefield around him, Ferlut, Gerdoise and Flambert were dead. Their bodies, slashed almost bare in parts, bore witness to the fury with which the dogs had charged on them.

Flambert, his sightless eyes turned up into his head, held in a muzzle clenched rigid in death the forefoot of a dog. He had fought himself out to the end, and, like his two brothers, had obeyed the ancient law of the wolves and died without a groan.

Fulmet, his loins mangled, was still propped upright by the tree he had had to back against. Blood was welling from broad wounds in his belly.

There was not a single wolf who was not wounded, and all were more or less finished for immediate action. But they could still use their legs, or at least drag themselves along. . . .

The one exception was Fulmet. His eyes were alert, but from the stiff manner in which he kept his unnatural sitting position by the tree, he seemed paralysed.

Among the boars, Dame Albaine's cousin Bougon had lost a tusk. The bears alone seemed to have come through

without serious injury. They bore traces enough of the
battle, but most of the blood that covered them was not
their own.

Panting and heaving, aware of the sudden flight of the
dogs but not yet appreciating if they would return, the
animals looked at each other with uncertainty. Hurlaud
rallied them.

'The column must have got through, comrades. But now it
is up to us to rejoin it, for it is virtually unprotected. And
we have another duty to face. Plantagenet will not be able
to last for ever, running circles round the horsemen. I am
afraid that we shall have to take them on, too. Pick yourselves up, men. Dust yourselves off. Prepare to march.'

There was a rattle from the throat of Fulmet. He seemed
to be making random experiments before stumbling on the
correct mode of communication.

'March without me,' Fulmet told the animals. 'I shall not
be able to keep up. All I should do would be to hold you
back, and you haven't a second to lose. If the dogs come back
I will take them on again and keep them busy just for a little.
Get going, brothers. Double up. Don't worry about me.'

Hurlaud went up to Fulmet. Baclin followed him. They
exchanged a glance. Fulmet the Great had had it. If the dogs
came back on the attack, he could not fight them off for
long, and he would have a terrible death.

Fulmet watched as his brothers silently took in the
situation. He spoke in a very calm voice:

'I haven't much more than an hour or two to go. I know
that. Finish me off. The pain is bad.'

Slowly he slid on to his side. A little stream of blood
gushed at the foot of the tree.

Animals have laws and secrets which they themselves
recognize without rationalizing. For them it is an honour to
die through the act of a friend, when there is nothing more
to hope for.

Hurlaud understood. He went a few paces away and then moved towards Flandrin. The bear seemed to know in advance what Hurlaud was asking. Without a word he went back with Hurlaud to the tree where Fulmet lay.

Seeing the bear in front of him, Fulmet gave him a feeble smile. 'Good old Flandrin,' he said. 'But do it quickly. The pain . . . you understand.'

Flandrin rasped in his throat, could not speak, and motioned to Hurlaud and Baclin to go back a few paces.

'Goodbye, dear friend,' he said in a choking voice. 'May God take you into his holy keeping.'

Then, with one swift blow, he felled Fulmet. The wolf made no sound. His limbs relaxed on the earth at the foot of the tree. With delicate accuracy Flandrin drew his claw through the carotid artery. Only a little blood came out. Fulmet the Great was dead.

It was a moment of deep emotion. Everyone kept a grave silence. Then, one by one, the animals came to sniff at the bodies of their fallen friends, who had died that all the rest might live. This is a service of homage that is always rendered in the secret world of the animals.

At the end of the brief ceremony Hurlaud recalled them to the urgencies of the moment, in a voice that showed total exhaustion. 'Follow me, my friends,' he said. 'The next stage will not be easy. Soon we shall have to break out of cover. We have a job to do. Let's get on with it.'

Not now in parade-ground order, but still at a steady pace, the animals took up the line of march of the main party, and followed it at the best possible speed.

At the time when the battle began Plantagenet, obeying Hurlaud's orders, had been rushing towards the astounded horsemen with twenty howling dogs at his heels. 'I can't believe it!' said one of the riders. 'Maister Brémand, look who's joining us! Surely that's your little pig that the dogs are hunting!'

'Oh, this is too much!' groaned Brémand. 'Those idiot curs are going to tear my poor Plantagenet to pieces. Of course that's Plantagenet, but what the devil is he doing here? Oh, the foolish, fond creature. He must have seen me leave the farm and no doubt decided to follow me. Call off those cretinous curs and give them the stick. Nothing must happen to Plantagenet, nothing. My daughter would die from the shock of it.'

Brémand squared his eyes as he tried to peer through the dawn mist. Then out of his throat there tore a great choking splutter that must have done him a serious internal injury. He had just recognized the leading dog. It was his own mastiff, the sinister Hargneu, who was heading the pack. Oaths of a sort never heard on earth before spat from his twisted lips as he tried to penetrate the dog's dim brain with epithets that would make him halt in terror. 'Blunderbaggery shiffossicating harrumminous Hargneu! Here, sir, here at once, sir, so I can tickle your sides, you jejammering bostical zamp! And you, you cretins!' he shouted to his flabbergasted horsemen. 'What are you waiting for? Rescue my pig. Keep that rabble of rat-catchers off my poor Plantagenet!'

The farm servants dug in their spurs and tried to get between Plantagenet and the dogs, who were pressing him hard. With his tail as stiff as ever at these moments of crisis, and squealing the old high cry of terror that he had been hoping he had grown out of, Plantagenet ran straight towards the approaching horses. Hargneu himself was so intoxicatingly crazed with his mounting lust of the chase that he had decided to treble his final pleasure by rubbing the itch and hissing a running commentary to his victim as the climax approached. He was like a headsman who not only wanted the condemned man to feel the axe he was about to wield, but turned him to face upwards on the block so that he could see the blade coming down. It was a mistake, for it expended good breath that would otherwise have sent more oxygen to the dog's muscles, and words cost yards.

'Slow down, sweetheart,' snarled Hargneu. 'I want to kiss your scraggy buttocks. One thing I promise you, and that's that you'll never sit down comfortably again in the short life that's left to you. Lord High-and-Mighty Grondin picked a quarrel with me about you. If he ever gets the chance to view the body of his cousin again, he'll notice some splendid scars on the rear.' Plantagenet was so moved by these startling menaces that he put up his highest screech of the day and gained a few paces, which inflamed Hargneu's rage so much that he stopped hissing. The dog was aware that he was the object of a remarkable series of curses from Maister Brémand that would have justified the projection of a new dictionary, but he did not really want to know. To catch this pernicious pig would be worth the sorriest beating. And one, more or less, made no difference.

Plantagenet had now been running for a long time and his pace was slackening. He sensed the jaws of Hargneu approaching. He tried to tack and make his pursuer lose ground, but it was a lost endeavour.

He gave a sudden, even more piercing cry that topped the note that was his previous record. Hargneu had just closed on the stiff tail which, contrary to all theories about the survival of the fittest, stuck out backwards like a ramrod. With infinite satisfaction the dog made a careful incision and skinned this long-suffering scut, then with a spasm of ecstasy made a bound and caught the tail to remove a further layer. Plantagenet made a desperate acceleration and dived amid the hooves of the advancing horses.

The confusion was indescribable, far better than Hurlaud could have hoped for. The horses reared, some of them threw their riders, the whole troop jarred to a halt. Amid shouting, neighing, and the less imaginative oaths which the peasants could always be relied on for, Plantagenet carved for himself

a difficult passage, still held at the tail by Hargneu. The rest
of the pack of dogs contributed to the shambles. Plantagenet
had anticipated being bitten and trampled. But he found that
the high tide of jaws and teeth, legs and hooves, came in
with an additional crest of pain. A dozen cudgels were being
vigorously swung by the horsemen to beat the dogs off
Plantagenet, and about half the blows aimed at the dogs
connected by mistake with the pig.

Intolerable noise, sharp pain and above all an overpower-
ing fear submerged Plantagenet into a peculiar state of
consciousness like a fevered delirium. He saw movement
which he did not immediately interpret. As if in a dream he
observed something like a feathered spear-head descending
and disappearing at extraordinary speed, passing and re-
passing but always coming in from above, always very fast,
and always favouring Plantagenet, by attacking whatever
dog, horse or man was persecuting him most severely at the
moment. Then his eye seemed to clear and he saw more
distinctly the swift plunging dive of a creature with beak
extended and all claws out, and he realized that Bafrin the
falcon was fighting for him.

Bafrin was keeping his word. With his razor-sharp beak
he was diving at the dogs, aiming for the eyes, and when the
head was averted his beak and claws tore at their spines. He
was using his speed to the utmost advantage, never stopping
to maul after the first tearing stab, never losing his momentum in that scrambling tumult to the point where he could
not extricate himself. Again and again he flew up high to
return like a whirlwind, digging his powerful talons into
whatever was most dangerous to Plantagenet in that instant.
Even the horsemen did not deter him, and they found they
had to defend themselves from his assaults. In that confused
battle the only envoy from the world of the forest to the
martyred Plantagenet could be Bafrin the Noble, and
suddenly Plantagenet knew that he was not abandoned.

'It's a falcon! Get that brute for God's sake,' shouted Henriot. 'Georges, your bow, quick!'

The man shot skilfully, but the bird succeeded in avoiding his shafts several times. The horsemen had now fixed their attention on the threat from the air, and in the remission of blows which was afforded Plantagenet tried to get nearer to Maister Brémand. Hargneu had been dislodged but still he tried to follow. Seeing what was happening, Bafrin dived straight towards Hargneu. An arrow took him in full whip, penetrating his flesh with a soft soughing sound. Plantagenet heard the cry of distress from his friend above him.

The beautiful bird fluttered, thrust up his head, and mounted. He flew steeply up, straight into the sky, to a height from which, for the last time, he would be granted a full sight of the dawn. He was no more than a dark speck in the grey when suddenly, majestic in death, he spread his great wings, hovered for a moment, and plunged without a cry into the waters of the Guirande, claiming for himself the final dignity of depriving the men and the dogs of his remains. Bafrin the Noble had paid the ransom for Plantagenet's deliverance, and Plantagenet had seen him fall. 'It should not be!' he groaned. 'That you should die for me.'

'Good shot, Georges!' cheered Henriot. 'Come on, you others. Get that pig away from the dogs.' He jumped to the ground, followed by Jacquet and Brémand. They strode into the snarling pack. Suddenly one of the horsemen gave a hoarse shout and pointed into the distance. There, at the edge of the forest, speeding into the plain was an entire column of animals. Brémand turned deathly pale. There were boars, wolves, bears, foxes and smaller beasts, shambling in a body at speed. 'To horse!' he yelled. 'Mount! Quick! There are the enemy. It's incredible! Cut off their retreat.' But he could get no order out of the tangled dogs

and maddened horses. He charged into the confusion
beating indiscriminately with his stick. He fell full length on
a heap of curs and pulled out Plantagenet from under them.
'Ah, my poor Plantagenet. What a dreadful condition
you're in. It's these wild beasts from the forest. They must
have come up on you and that is why you were in flight.
And then these wretched dogs fastened on you. You idiot
curs! Why can't you leave this poor creature alone?' He
lashed out in fury with his cudgel. In his blind rage he was
not entirely accurate, and some of the blows fell on Plantagenet. In complete bewilderment Plantagenet could only
conclude that the humans had somehow discovered his part
in the planned escape of the animals, and for this treason he
was going to be lynched on the spot. In desperate self-
preservation he snapped with his teeth at any flesh within
reach, made a gap, and darted into the free space. Hargneu
tried to follow him, but Brémand nailed him to the ground
with his cudgel. Plantagenet seized his opportunity, hurled
himself into the air, landed on his feet and raced away into
the distance.

'Wolves!' yelled a horseman. 'They're following the
others!' Brémand looked up and saw Hurlaud's group
passing in its turn from the forest on to the plain. 'To
horse!' he shouted again. 'By God at least we can get these!
Come on, you sots, hurry, get at the wolves. But where are
the hounds that took them on?'

'There!' said Henriot. The pack that had fought the
wolves was slinking towards the men in small, utterly
beaten groups. Brémand could not believe his eyes. Every
surviving hound was bleeding with savage wounds.

Brémand thought fast as he reviewed the situation. With
the few working dogs that remained to him he had less
chance of overcoming the wolves. And to continue the
action now would risk upsetting the whole time-table of the
battue by a late arrival for the rendezvous at the castle of

Crespin. But he could not endure the shame of giving up. 'I still have you,' he said to Rupert, who was waiting at his heels. 'And so far Hargneu and his pack have taken on nothing but a pig.' He threw himself into the saddle. 'Forward!' he shouted. All the horsemen and the sound dogs remaining rushed in pursuit of the wolves.

Plantagenet was running, now almost literally flying, towards the farmstead at La Tranchée.

Hurlaud and his friends had a good five hundred paces' advantage on the nearest horsemen. That would have been a useful lead if nothing had happened beforehand. But many of the normally speedy wolves were wounded and exhausted, and the other animals were very slow. There was no question of abandoning Flandrin and the bears, and all the Boulet family who had come so bravely to their rescue. All were a pitiful sight to see. Hurlaud himself had to check his pace from time to time to lick the blood which gushed from his skull on to his cheeks. At these moments he took the opportunity to call out encouragement to his troop. 'Only a few minutes, and we'll reach Les Fosses. Hang on, my friends.' He slackened his speed so that Flandrin could come up with him. 'Keep going, Monseigneur,' he exhorted the exhausted bear.

The horsemen pursuing them drew nearer. There was still half a league to go. But the sight of the first clumps of trees gave new endurance to the fugitives. Hurlaud told Baclin to lead on the last stretch, while he drifted to the tail of the column, which was now highly vulnerable. 'Don't let yourself be over-run,' he told Flandrin, 'or you will be lost. Whatever happens I'll stay with you. But, Lord, we're not going to die so feebly.' Flandrin managed a grin. He had just heard, above the sound of the galloping horses behind, the clattering of lances as they were eased from their rests. A moment later a spear plunged into the ground on Hurlaud's right.

'Start weaving, Monseigneur,' said Hurlaud. 'Broaden the distance between us, then tack from side to side.' They separated, but kept abreast of each other. Hurlaud willed himself to keep his speed down to Flandrin's lumbering gait but at his natural pace he was constantly shooting ahead.

The clumps of trees were almost within reach. Baclin had just dived into them. 'The horsemen will never risk themselves in the forest in such small numbers,' Hurlaud told himself. 'From the moment we are in the wood we shall be able to turn and face them.' A howl brought him back to the reality of the moment. He suddenly saw Flandrin dash past him with a spear embedded in his left flank. Hurlaud put on speed. Spears were landing in the ground not only around him but several paces in front. He heard the whistle of one in flight and bounded to one side as it hit the line of his old course. Flandrin was losing blood and panting with exhaustion, but he was coming up to the first trees. He charged straight into a thicket and left the spear-shaft caught in the branches, its head dripping with a patch of his flesh torn from his body. Hurlaud saw a narrow path ahead of him and turned for a moment before deciding to take it. He saw hooves two paces behind him, swiftly swerved and dived into thick bushes. The horse continued on the track and a low branch swept the rider from his saddle.

Brémand reined in his horse and ordered the others to disengage. There was no point in prolonging the pursuit and confronting the wolves in their natural element. And he could no longer risk missing the rendezvous with Messire de Frébois. Cursing with vexation he turned his horse and rode with his companions as fast as possible on the track towards the castle.

A few paces away, where the trees were already dense, Baclin, Boulet and the others had already taken up defensive positions and were poised to jump at the throat of anyone who decided to take the battle farther. Hurlaud and Flandrin joined them, and they relaxed in a silence broken only by their heavy, painful breathing. After a short time Hurlaud rallied them and, though he was now almost too crippled to walk, led them along the path from Les Fosses towards Chizé. At a spot already agreed, between two ancient oaks, Grondin's uncle, Rohart, was waiting. He was a veteran warrior, still vigorous, mild-mannered but with a look of undisputed authority in his eye. Without a gesture or a sound he watched as the limping rearguard approached. When Hurlaud came up with him they exchanged one keen glance and Rohart made a slight bow. 'I was waiting for you, brothers. I am very relieved to see you here. The best news you could give me would be that you have suffered no losses, but I fear there may be cause for my grief, which I ask you to believe is as deep as yours. I give you the freedom of our forest, and if its riches do not compare with what you have left, it is at all events less hazardous. Be pleased to regard it as yours, and may you find in it peace and rest.'

Hurlaud, covered with blood, his yellow eyes blazing under his grey brow, bowed in his turn. 'I am deeply grateful to you, Monseigneur, for giving us such a courteous welcome. Some of our company, and they among the best of us, have paid with their lives in order that we should have the pleasure of joining you in your domain. Our thoughts go to them, our deference to you. We shall follow you, Monseigneur, wherever you wish.'

Rohart bowed again and led the column at a pace suited to their condition. As he went along he passed on the news: 'Your families have come through, unscathed as far as I am aware, except that some marcassins and young cubs have strayed. My brother Puthet has gone out with a scouting party, and should be able to whip them in without too much trouble. There has been no occurrence of great gravity, except what has happened to yourselves.'

Hurlaud thanked him with a simple inclination of his head. He had no more strength to call on for a more formal reply.

16
The Capitulation

The arrival of Maister Brémand and his party at the castle caused a great stir. Messire de Frébois welcomed his guests on the front steps, and was amazed to see them in such a dishevelled state. He was even more concerned when he saw the dogs. He immediately instructed servants to dress their wounds and try and restore some spirit in them. At some length Brémand recounted all the events of the morning. Messire de Frébois was completely confounded. 'What are you telling me, Brémand? This is very alarming. It could well be that the number of animals you have seen makes up the total strength of the predators in the forest. If these cursed brutes have managed to get into the depths of Chizé, our entire plans for the day will be no more effective than a sword thrust into water. Devil take it, these brutes are not endowed with *thought*! Have I to believe that this was all done by instinct? An operation like this battue can never be duplicated at Chizé. We should need three times the number of men, and we have already denuded the hamlets. In any case, judging by the state of your dogs, these brutes are prepared to make a fight of it. How many have you lost?'

'About twenty,' said Henriot mournfully.

'Incredible!' said Messire de Frébois. 'Well, we shall soon have the proof of it. We shall come up on the battlefield and I suppose we shall find plenty of bodies. Well, action,

action. Come into the hall, friends, I have a hot meal prepared for you, but eat quickly, I beg you, for we must be off.'

Very shortly afterwards the imposing battle array so carefully organized by Messire de Frébois moved out of the castle gate to take up the dispositions previously planned. The beaters, under the orders of Monsieur Jehan, took up their station on the terrain between Donkey Bottom and La Fiallerie. Behind them were ranged the men-at-arms, and as the force moved forward they marched at the qui vive, bows bent and pikes at the ready. The horsemen kept station in the rear. The time-table envisaged that the beaters should halt at about noon, and squat for an open-air meal and a rest, holding the line with the footmen while the knights repaired for midday dinner at La Tranchée, which would be near the front to which the forces from Crespin should have advanced. The victuals for the beaters were being carried on the march, and the provisions for the others had already been installed in La Tranchée. The closing of the square through the junction with the forces of Messires des Golletières, des Chaussées and the Seneschal was timed for four o'clock. The systematic comb-out after the battue was calculated to occupy the rest of that day and all the next.

At about nine o'clock the beaters reached the site of the battle between Hurlaud's forces and the dogs. Amid great excitement the bodies of Ferlut, Gerdoise, Flambert and Fulmet were carried to Messire de Frébois, and the disembowelled and butchered corpses of eighteen dogs were recovered. De Frébois inspected the battlefield. Gloomily he repeated his fears about the outcome of the battue. Up to that moment no beater had put up any animal except game and birds. Already they were beginning to show impatience. With no wild life to occupy them they were working much faster than had been scheduled, and at intervals they were ordered to halt in order to keep down to the

time-table set for the other teams in the square forming the
battue. 'Not a wolf, not a badger, not a boar, not even a
heron,' fumed Maister Jacquet. 'Have we got to believe that
they've all run the other way to surrender to Messire des
Golletières?'

'Patience, patience,' said Messire de Frébois in a very
unconvinced and unconvincing tone.

Noon came, and still not one beast among their quarry
had appeared. In undisguised bad temper everyone stopped
for the angelus prayer. La Tranchée was only a short distance away. Hampers of food, crocks of wine and sides of ·
country ham were brought up for the footmen, and the
horsemen galloped off to the farm.

As soon as he had dismounted Messire de Frébois paid
Maister Brémand the expected honour of going round the
farmstead, duly expressed himself as very satisfied with the
excellent condition of the place, and warmly congratulated
Brémand. During the tour the guests passed in front of the
pig-sty. It was empty. Frowning at the open door, Brémand
seemed troubled. 'Lord bless us, Messire,' he said, 'those
wretched curs must have injured my poor Plantagenet
badly. It would be a terrible thing if . . . if. . . . My Adèle
would never get over it.'

'What do you mean? Has your daughter made a friend of
this pig?'

'Yes,' Brémand admitted with some embarrassment.
'And I must say that everyone else here has done the same.
He's no ordinary animal, you know. Ask Monsieur Jehan
his opinion.' With many superfluous details Jehan recited
what he had seen the previous evening, and got the explosion
of laughter he had been playing for when he came to the
point of the fall into the tub of water. Then everyone went
to the great room of the farm, which had been decorated
with ivy for the occasion. After paying lavish compliments
to the ladies of the house Messire de Frébois took his place

of honour at the dinner. The famous wine of Maister Brémand circulated freely. The frustrations of the morning began to dissolve. The happy chatter, the peals of laughter, the roars of applause after each toast, could clearly be heard in the courtyard, and even reached the ears of the knackered pig Plantagenet, deeply embedded in the straw inside a barn.

Plantagenet had arrived, bloody and bruised, in a state of complete exhaustion. He had only two thoughts in his mind: first, he must not let Adèle suffer the shock of seeing him in this state, yet somehow he wanted to re-assure her that he was still her brother Plantagenet – and a live Plantagenet; second, he had to rest as effectively as possible in order to restore himself for the next round of the fight, which he could not think had yet reached its decisive climax. Since there were no able-bodied manservants left on the farm, with only a very old man deputed to watch the main gate, and since all the women had gone back to bed for a couple of hours, having been up at three o'clock and facing the prospect of serving a massive banquet at midday, Plantagenet got into La Tranchée entirely unobserved, the decrepit porter being also asleep. Plantagenet made a quick raid on the pantry and discovered a truly royal selection of food. Having satisfied himself, for once without any thought for his figure, he looked around for a titbit he could present to Adèle. He paused before a particularly succulent sausage, but a faint suggestion of cannibalism decided him to reject it. He chose an extremely fine pâté en croûte and carefully carried it to Adèle's bedroom, leaving it outside the door. Then, instead of going to his own sty, he sneaked into the barn and burrowed very deeply into a seductively high pile of straw. He slept like a lord until the boisterous cheering from the great room awakened him, and at the same time he realized that he was once more in mortal danger from the old enemy. Chaos had come again.

The dogs, who had followed their masters to the farm, had flopped down with their usual indolence as soon as they arrived. Gradually one or two of the more fidgety ne'er-do-wells began to ferret about the courtyard. They picked up the pig's scent. One of them slipped into the hole which Plantagenet had made, found an indication of his prey, and gave tongue. Soon all the dogs were rummaging feverishly in the barn, making the straw fly in all directions. In desperation Plantagenet began to crawl even further inside the stack. He was seized by a trailing trotter and was triumphantly dragged out into the open. The hubbub had attracted Hargneu, lord of the curs. He strode to inspect the scene. What a windfall! Not only could he present his final account to the accursed pig, but since it was well known that all the pack had had a feud with Plantagenet, Hargneu could dodge any accusation of having put the porker to death. At the same time, he was resolved that no one else should purloin that pleasure. All that he was offering the others was a taste of the spoil and a share of the blame. 'Come on, you chaps,' he called matily to the dogs, 'if you don't make a meal of this fellow there'll be nothing to show for the day. Don't expect too much from the Messieurs. They'll only leave you bones to nibble and dirty bowls to lick. At least let's get something out of this battue. We'll rid ourselves of this traitor once and for all, and at the end of it we'll have a taste in our mouths which will be rather better than the dishwater we can expect from Them in the Hall.

'Now kindly clear a path,' he enunciated with mounting inebriation at the prospect before him. 'Gangway, gangway, if you please. You are now about to witness the model Hexecution of all time. A proper Hexecution if ever there was one. All good traditional stuff, gentlemen, prolonged and persistent torture like Grandad used to mix it, none of your bland namby-pamby modern taste for mercy here. Based on the original Chinese death of a thousand cuts, but refined with elaborate excruciation such as only a French artist could conceive.

'Stage one: I shall now proceed to frighten the prisoner while at the same time introducing myself by name so that no one will be able to doubt the authenticity of this work of art. Hargneu! *Hargneu!* HARGNEU!'

The sound was rolling from his throat, very low in pitch, very loud in volume, very pulsating as if a corrugated saw was being drawn across his larynx. It was a masterpiece of an artistic signature, and Plantagenet, who was naturally listening with great interest, understood that *Hargneu* was not just the name of his persecutor, it was the aboriginal, primeval, palaeozoic snarl of all time. HARGNEU! HARGNEU! HARGNEU!

Plantagenet had indeed been reacting to this harangue in a quite extraordinary manner, and Hargneu was a little careless, or too absorbed in his art, or perhaps just plain dim, not to have noticed it. The dog might have been wiser not to have indulged in his fairground barking, for it was during this speech that the great change materialized. At the beginning Plantagenet had presented a self-portrait of piteous terror. He was silent, shrinking, pathetic, and his eyes had changed to a blue colour with the appeal of a helpless baby. As the dog's exultation mounted Plantagenet's fear and physical impotence seemed to increase to such a point that he might have been suspected of wilful exaggeration.

Now Hargneu braced himself to spring, and Plantagenet was shrinking even smaller. The dog bounded like a ball of stone from a Roman ballista, and suddenly Plantagenet stood up straight with his head extended. His snout opened and he sank his teeth into Hargneu's oncoming breast, closed them, and shook the dog with incredible violence, from side to side, again and again, finally tossing his enemy into a heap of dung. Plantagenet breathed deeply and his body expanded, seeming to gain additional size from the bristling of all his hairs. He gave a terrible roar which bore no relation at all to any sound any pig had ever uttered. In instinctive fear the crowd of mastiffs shrank back. Plantagenet charged the nearest group, rolled them over, and shot like an arrow through the courtyard.

'After him!' shrieked Hargneu, writhing in pain. 'Catch him!' Hargneu bounded forward but his fore legs bore on the newly-torn muscles in his chest, and he collapsed with his jaws in the dust. 'Get after that pig!' Hargneu again yelled to his pack, blowing clouds of chaff with his breath. 'Taquin, you're in charge.' But before the pack had recovered its senses Plantagenet had already crossed the porch and was racing in the direction of the forest. The dogs followed, baying with the renewed vacuous enthusiasm of those who never learn from experience.

'What's all that row?' asked Messire de Frébois in the middle of a mouthful of roast.

'It's just those gutless curs letting us know they're hungry,' said Maister Brémand, lowering a thick slice of beef into Rupert's jaws, delicately so that the gravy would not run down his chops. 'I shall never forgive them for that idiot attack on Plantagenet, and even now I don't know what they've done to him. They can just wait for their food, that's all. Do tell me your opinion of this wine, Messire. It's a vintage from Les Grosses Terres. A little different from the last one you tasted. Perhaps a trifle provocative. . . .'

The start Plantagenet had gained was more than enough. He was back to flying form and he was thinking coolly. It had been a brilliant idea to return to La Tranchée. He had completed his diversionary tactic with the extra five minutes' hullabaloo which saved Hurlaud and Flandrin; he had convinced Brémand that he was only a poor innocent victim of mindless farm dogs, rather than an architect of the defeat of the battue; he had taken a soldier's privilege of snatching a snack and a snooze as soon as it was convenient;

and now he had a couple of dozen hounds out again volunteering for exercise which would do the afternoon shift of the battue no service at all. To give them a more exhausting run, Plantagenet headed through the forest as though going to Les Combles, then made a détour towards Stags Crossing, then doubled back towards the plain, and was eventually following the path which the column of animals had taken earlier that morning. In this manner he led the dogs to Les Fosses and the outskirts of the great forest of Chizé.

Within the depths of this forest the main body of the animals was now safe, small family parties being guided to appropriate spots by Rohart's scouts. On the near edge of the forest Grondin was at that moment organizing his defence line. Hurlaud had come back from his official reception by Rohart to help in deploying the defence. But Grondin had, after very long persuasion, convinced the wolf that his wounds were too severe to merit any treatment other than prolonged rest. Hurlaud had therefore very recently withdrawn to make his way back to the attentions of Dame Pernale.

Grondin planned a nutcracker defence using Flandrin and his brother bears as the main static bastion, with Bursiat and a strong force of boars as the leg of the nutcracker, ready to swing in sharply and trap opponents battering at the almost invulnerable bears. Swift communications were to be maintained by Fulgent, Fléton and other foxes.

Flandrin and Bursiat were agreeing details when they heard the baying of the pack in pursuit of Plantagenet.

'Sooner than we thought,' said Flandrin with a laugh. 'Take up your positions,' he called to the bears. 'We are going to have visitors, and by the blood of the Great Bear we must receive them worthily.' Immediately, everyone hid in the bushes on each side of the path. The sound of the dogs was now louder, but well ahead of them, as it seemed, came the pounding gallop of their quarry. Grondin looked out into the plain. Suddenly he saw Plantagenet, his head between his shoulders, his eyes set on the forest, his legs criss-crossing like trellises.

Grondin did not expect to see his cousin again so soon. His conclusion was that either Plantagenet was a herald of bad news or else he was in danger of death. Fortunately his cousin still held a long enough lead over the pack for Grondin to be able to deal with either eventuality.

Grondin moved out of a thicket and stood in Plantagenet's path. 'Take it easy, Plantagenet. What's the hurry?'

'Ah, it's you, cousin Grondin. Look out for yourself. I have the whole pack from the seigneurie of Frébois on my heels.'

'Excellent,' said Grondin. 'They've saved us the trouble of a rehearsal. We were just going to have a TEWT.'

'What's a TEWT?'

'Tactical Exercise Without Troops. TEWT, you newt. No time to explain now. Just sham dead in the middle of the path, will you?'

'Sham dead?'

'Yes.'

'Are you sure I'll be shamming in two minutes' time? I'm not a very good actor.'

'You didn't do so badly playing Grondin opposite Hargneu the other day. Why this false modesty when we're in a hurry? Sham dead and stop arguing. I'm going to disappear.'

'You'll come back?'

'Of course I'll come back. I told you we've abandoned the TEWT, you newt.'

Plantagenet lay in the middle of the path, and composed himself just as the hounds poured round a bend.

'There he is! Come on. We've got him.'

The dogs came bounding towards Plantagenet. Grondin

burst from the brushwood and planted himself between them and their quarry, facing the entire pack. With a scoop of his snout Grondin caught the leading dog and sent him rolling into the middle of his mates, throwing them all off balance.

Seeing Grondin in the middle of the clearing, the dogs stopped their pursuit and consulted together. They were numerous enough to have the boar at their mercy. The strongest amongst them came to the front, creeping, gliding on the damp ground, uttering low growls heavy with menace. Muscles stretched, backs arched, they prepared to attack. Behind them the others followed, slightly hesitant but convulsively rolling back their lips. Grondin did not stir. He openly stared at the biggest mastiff, who had withdrawn to one side to attack him from the flank.

The mastiff's attention was caught by a slight movement to his right. There, sitting up against a tree almost as if he were a squirrel, completely at ease with his arms folded, was Fulgent the fox, laughing his head off.

'You know Grondin, of course,' he said sociably to the astounded dogs. 'I don't think you've met Bursiat, Théclot, Vanlis and Fourrier.'

Four huge black shapes appeared out of the undergrowth behind Grondin. They were Bursiat and his companion boars, three blood brothers of Dame Albaine.

'Hilfred de Chizé, his brother Hémon, Jurmi and Parnaud des Fosses,' said Fulgent effecting further introductions. 'Urbain the Hermit, Ulrich the Devil, Pumard and three friends whose names for the moment escape me. I have not long had the honour of their acquaintance.'

Nine more black boars came out from the undergrowth on either side of the dogs. The tenth, Ulrich, was disfigured by gross patches of white on his hide. He was believed by the others to practise sorcery as a private hobby.

'Not to speak of Flandrin and his very large and capable family,' concluded Fulgent.

The dogs saw no further movement to match this last introduction. Then they followed the direction of Fulgent's eyes. Behind them, cutting off all escape, Flandrin was advancing, walking on his hind feet, his nostrils frothing, his jaws dribbling with pain and rage, his wound of that morning showing dark red on his flank where the blood had clotted. With him were an awesome company of bears, too many to be counted at one glance, led by Flandrin's younger brother Hériet and his mother Turonde, grizzled with age but moving with the sinister menace of an old Amazon.

The dogs, who had begun to turn to make a desperate sortie of escape, at last understood the situation. Not one would get out of this trap alive. They began to circle desperately, bristling, one treading on another, uttering cries of fear. One dog, in an all-or-nothing effort, made a dash under the thicket to the left of Bursiat. A howl of agony was followed by the death-rattle. Others were on guard behind Bursiat. The grey head of Melheu the wolf appeared, loosing an evil grin. In spite of the morning encounter, when he had almost lost a paw, he intended to be in at the death.

The circle narrowed more and more. Soon the stupefied dogs could smell all around them the strong breath of the wild animals.

'Come, comrades, let's get it over,' called Grondin, lowering his head and preparing to charge.

At that moment a cracked but peremptory voice sounded from behind the boars. It was Hurlaud, warned by Fléton the fox, who had left the rearguard party as soon as the ambush had been formed. Hurlaud was dragging himself rather than walking. His back was red with dried blood and his ears were in shreds. He came up to Grondin, who was clearly put out to be halted like this as he was about to charge.

'Come in, friend,' said Flandrin uneasily. 'Stand by me and take your share in this little chore. But you were fighting all morning and your wounds are caked. Why re-open them? Stand down now, and leave this to us. It's just a mopping-up operation.'

Hurlaud passed Grondin and limped up to Plantagenet. He stopped. Then, in a very clear voice which all the dogs could hear, he spoke with simple dignity:

'Ah, Plantagenet! You have re-joined us. Not without scars, it seems. Blood has been shed today, and yours has flowed as freely as any. I testify now to the admiration and respect I feel for you. It is you who have saved us, Plantagenet. It is thanks to your courage that all who lived in the forest and were forced to flee are now out of danger. You are one of us, Plantagenet. What can we offer you except to share our life? You may think that it is not much to give you. We are stalked, we are hunted, encircled by men-at-arms, physically trapped. Steel is levelled at our flesh as long as we live. What then is our gift? Only that you will be free, Plantagenet, free of subservience to a master, free from the stick in his hand. As far as in us lies we extend to you our devoted protection. Never will we let any man come near you, not even Messire de Frébois himself – or by my faith, by the pledge of Hurlaud des Grands Bois, he will find out the cost.'

He did not wait for a response, but went back to Grondin and addressed the concourse of animals like a king in parliament moving on to discuss the next measure.

'I suggest it would be wiser at this moment, my friends, to bargain from strength. It would be a simple matter to ensure that none of these curs escapes. But in that event we must expect, in my opinion, to have this whole organized battue shifted to fall on our backs here within two or three days. The alternative is to consider releasing some of them – perhaps all, if we obtain from them what we may call, let us say . . . guarantees.'

Hurlaud paused for some time to regain his strength. He was breathing stertorously. The effort of speech was draining his resources.

'I therefore propose that we let these kennel-bred scum go and be hanged elsewhere, on the express condition that they solemnly promise, one and all, in front of us here present, never again to trouble the peace of the forest which has been ours since the creation of the world. Not only are they to make that promise, but they are to renounce participation in any hunting expeditions organized by their wretched masters and their lackeys. They are to stay on their own ground, which was indeed once our territory before men annexed it, and cut it out of the forest, and imposed on it a law which we reject. They are to stay in their domain, which we hereby concede to them with its perpetual sanction of the rope and the stick. And finally,' he added in a voice now approaching exhaustion, 'even on this territory, which once was ours, they are not to take up any nocturnal pursuit of us if occasionally hunger forces us to make an incursion on the rich land which day by day flaunts its opulence and its reserves against the hand-to-mouth existence which all who live by Nature's seasons must observe.'

Hurlaud could hardly keep himself erect any longer. 'Are you agreed, my friends?' he asked. Without waiting for an answer he sank to the ground.

By every instinct Grondin was opposed to acceptance of Hurlaud's proposal. He tore at the ground with his hoof, then turned and consulted his companions with a glance.

There was a long and heavy silence. The eyes of the dogs continually flashed around the circle enclosing them as they waited for their fate to be decided.

After an intense period of frowning reflection, Flandrin spoke:

'What you have said, Hurlaud, is very reasonable. I have no doubt that you have no more trust than I have that these guttersnipes will keep their promise for long. Too bad. I deprive myself of a piece of action I had been rather looking forward to, but you are certainly right: the one thing we do not want to do is to bring down the attention of the men who hate us so much on our hosts here at Chizé who up to this time have lived in peace.'

Grondin spoke, still trying to keep up his bad temper, but with cheerfulness breaking through: 'As far as I am concerned, I want one more clause in the oath: that whatever Plantagenet's decision about where he lives, this verminous riff-raff swear to let him idle wherever he pleases, here or there, without offering him the least harm.'

'That goes without saying,' said Hurlaud.

All the other beasts of the forest nodded approval.

'The difficulty now is to find a reliable spokesman among this rabble,' said Hurlaud, turning contemptuously to the dogs. 'Is there any one among you with enough authority to speak for the others and enough integrity to take an oath that will be kept? We in the forest have the tradition that the oldest is listened to first. I understand that among your masters, and therefore in your own estimation, less respect is paid to age and experience than to power. Might is right. The bully is baron. You, Taquin, you seemed about to say something,' he observed to the dog Hargneu had nominated as his deputy.

'No, not me,' muttered Taquin.

'Yes, you. You speak. Taquin should speak,' murmured a number of the other dogs, grovelling for a decision.

After some hesitation Taquin advanced slightly out of the ranks of the dogs, more dead than alive. 'If it has to be me,' he said, 'I have to point out that I can take the oath you are proposing only in the name of the dogs of the farmstead of Maister Jacquet. I do not know the other dogs, and cannot see how the oath would bind them.'

'We commission you to act for us,' said dogs from the other farms. 'You have our mandate. Take the oath. It is binding on us.'

Taquin sighed, swallowed hard, then promised on his honour in the individual names of the pack there present that all the demands formulated by Hurlaud would be respected.

Hurlaud nodded grimly and addressed the hangdog crew: 'You dogs will be aware that you and your kind are the lowest of the animal world. You were the first beasts to be domesticated by man, and under his training you have become as disgusting as man. You tried to kill us, not because you were hungry or to save your own lives, but because it pleased men to have us killed, and you were . . . obedient. Now you have sworn an undertaking. Let not a single one of you forget that if this oath is broken, even by a solitary individual, we shall have you all, without pity or reprieve, one after the other.'

He turned to Flandrin. 'Let them out by the back door,' he said. Flandrin and the bears stood aside, and the dogs turned and loped out in silence. Never had hunting hounds been so humiliated. Completely cowed, they returned to La Tranchée, from where they could at least perform with a clear conscience in the second act of the farce of the battue.

When they were gone Hurlaud seemed to be fired with a little more spirit. 'I'm a sucker for the happy ending,' he said. 'Now I've laid on a party at Chizé and naturally you're all invited. Hah abaht thee, Plantagenet? Art tha coming wi' us, tha bugger?'

Plantagenet was entirely overcome. *Tha bugger!* Hurlaud had distinctly said it to him, it was promotion on the field, and they were now on terms of intimacy. He staggered with shock. This might be the accolade but it felt more like the pole-axe. Then Plantagenet pulled himself together, caught up with the moving column, and fell in step alongside his illustrious comrade and friend, Hurlaud of the Great Woods.

17
The Search

The journey into the forest took longer than they had anticipated. Their day had begun long before dawn and had included many leagues of marching besides the exertion of the battle. They were finally swinging along in a rhythmic jogtrot which banished all reasoning about exhaustion to frontiers beyond the trance they had induced in themselves. Eventually they came to the heart of the clearing of Paitout, and they were welcomed with an immense ovation. After the first extravagant effusions were over Hurlaud and Grondin went to the dens which had been prepared for them by their hosts. Grondin found that Dame Albaine was not there but the marcassins, who seemed greatly troubled, said she was with Dame Pernale. Grondin hurried to Hurlaud's place. He found the two mothers in tears. Puthet, the leader of the party sent by Rohart to round up the youngsters who had gone astray in the stampede crossing the plain, had returned without Pielet, the mischievous marcassin whom Grondin and Albaine had had to correct so often, and without Barthus, the most delicate of Dame Pernale's last litter of cubs. These were the only two who were missing from the final muster.

Puthet, a handsome, hard-working hulk of a boar even if he was not notably brilliant in intellect, was standing by Dame Albaine, exhausted by his search and embarrassed by his failure. 'I have brought in some twenty youngsters,' he said. 'What I cannot do is scour the fields around the Guirande without attracting attention which would be most dangerous for any survivors, for the plain is alive with beaters and spearmen. I have no doubt that your two youngsters are dug in somewhere and dare not budge – and their instinct is right, for it is best not to show themselves. If you think they are in the hollows on the farther side of the plain, which is more your country, I am very willing to have another search, but I do suggest that one of you goes out with me – or preferably,' he added hurriedly, after taking a long look at Hurlaud and Grondin, 'one of your party who is less exhausted than you.'

Hurlaud got up clumsily and made to follow Puthet. Daylight was beginning to fade. In an hour it would be night. 'Hurry up, Grondin,' said Hurlaud, 'we still have time.'

But the wolf was visibly staggering. 'Stay here, friend,' said Grondin. 'It will be a miracle if you get out there at all, and if you fall across three or four wandering dogs it will be the end. I'll go with Puthet and Baclin.'

'Baclin does not know that part of the plain,' said Hurlaud.

'Baclin has a good and accurate nose and can be a great help to us,' said Grondin.

'Go and fetch Baclin,' said Hurlaud curtly to one of his cubs.

'You're about the only one left among the fighter-wolves with enough strength left to stand up,' Grondin told Baclin when he came. 'Well, Melheu, too, perhaps. But you don't know the bends in the river and the meadow-borders in the Les Fosses area which is the ground that has to be particularly searched.'

Baclin thought for a moment, then said straight out:

'There's only one extra chap we need, and I don't know

why you haven't mentioned him. We've got to have Plantagenet.'

Grondin started up indignantly. 'Come off it, friend, haven't you seen the state he's in? He's bruised and bitten all over, he hasn't a hair on his hide, and he can't even sit down without agony.'

'He won't need to sit down,' said Baclin. 'All he has to do is to run, and believe me, he still does that very well.'

'Go and fetch Plantagenet,' said Grondin glumly to the cub who was running the messages.

Replete after a feast of acorns, Plantagenet was reclining on a velvety bed when he received the summons. He turned up immediately, dapper and spruce, making gracious bows to the unhappy parents and putting himself at their service with an extravagance of flourishes that he diminished only when he realized the depth of their crisis. As soon as he understood the mission he fixed Baclin with a steady eye. 'En route, Monsieur,' he said. 'We have little time.'

'I am coming with you,' said Grondin, 'and Baclin is bringing Melheu.' Hurlaud managed to hold out until he had seen his friends off, and then he collapsed under the gravity of his wounds.

Plantagenet swiftly led the way to the edge of the forest. From there they looked out over the plain towards the Guirande. 'When we reached the river,' said Grondin, 'the column was still in good order. It was afterwards that it broke up in the stampede. Dame Albaine tells me that many little ones were trampled on and began to flee in panic back towards the river.'

'Then that is where we start searching,' said Baclin. 'To be absolutely sure, let's get as far as the bridge and work backwards.'

'It will soon be night,' said Plantagenet. 'We must work fast.' And he set off at a furious pace towards the bridge.

'Devil take him, I have a game fore-foot,' grumbled Melheu. 'Or has the Devil taken him already?'

'You should be glad he hasn't a pack at his heels,' laughed Baclin. 'We wouldn't see him for dust.'

They searched the groves and thickets from the bridge at Souligné as far as the hedges bordering the farmland of Maister Jacquet. Baclin and Melheu, who both had a remarkable sense of smell, carefully combed both sides of the river. 'Nothing. It's always nothing,' groaned Baclin. 'Where have those two fellows earthed up?' An evening mist was now spreading over the plain, which did not help matters at all.

Grondin was visibly being racked by anguish at this stage. Plantagenet seemed unshakeable. 'I'll bring those prodigal sons back to the fold again,' he kept assuring Grondin. They explored the top hedge of the Fanon meadow from one end to the other, without result. Baclin uttered a dispirited curse. Suddenly Plantagenet's ears went flat, a sign which Grondin had learned to interpret as either keen attention or intense fear. The pig sniffed the air for a moment and charged across the Fanon meadow like a mad bull. The others followed as best they could. Plantagenet stopped behind the second hedge at the bottom of the field. The river ballooned into a lazy bend here and had flooded the bank, leaving an alluvial deposit topped with a jumble of flotsam, dead wood and a foul-smelling spongy residue. Behind a tree stump, absolutely motionless and rolled into a ball, Pielet and Barthus were ineffectively hiding. Two paces in front of them, but with his back to them, was Rupert the beagle. Opposite Rupert, grimacing with rage and hate, was Hargneu, the abominable Hargneu.

The cur had not had a good day, although he had escaped the humiliation of the ambush and the oath of neutrality through the immediate effect of the bite Plantagenet had reserved for him. When the battue was resumed Hargneu publicly pilloried Taquin for cowardice in the face of the enemy by taking the oath proposed by Hurlaud. When challenged, he could not suggest an alternative reaction, but gave a sneering reminder that he was not bound by the promise. There was no effective test of whether the rest of the pack considered themselves bound by their oath or not, since not a single wild animal was put up for them to demonstrate their state of mind on. At around four o'clock, as planned, the junction of all the forces was effected when the square closed at Les Combles, and beaters, huntsmen and horsemen realized that they had never laid themselves open to such ridicule in their lives. Messire de Frébois hurriedly tried to quell any sense of mutiny by inviting everyone to drown their sorrows at the castle of Crespin. When the castle came in sight Hargneu slipped away with hate in his heart and a determination to make someone – preferably Plantagenet if he could be found – pay dear for the misfortunes of the day. Rupert, suspecting some act of unprovoked aggression, had also dropped out of the column and followed at a distance, for he was convinced that if Hargneu came across Plantagenet in the black rage that then dominated him, it would be all up with his friend. Hargneu had ranged the river bank without success. Then quite by accident he fell across Pielet and Barthus, who fled in terror to earth up behind the dead stump. Slobbering and howling, Hargneu prepared for the kill. There was small physical risk in taking on in the open a wolf cub and a yearling young boar. If he took back their remains to the castle he could achieve pardon of a sort from Maister Brémand for his previous escapades. And he would gain that vital prestige among the other dogs that he needed since the death that day of Muquon, an event that opened up for him vast doors in his hopes for the hierarchy of the future.

All these pleasant ambitions were brusquely clouded by the sudden appearance of the English beagle Rupert, who had dashed from the river and barred his way. Hargneu, who had always hated this stuck-up foreigner, could not hide his rage. And that was what Plantagenet, who was very familiar with the low snarling of his enemy, had been alone in hearing from the edge of Fanon meadow.

'You're in my way,' growled Hargneu.

'How frightfully inconvenient for you,' said Rupert, wilfully exaggerating his English accent because it annoyed Hargneu. 'Try and move me. Ectually I'm demmed elusive.'

Hargneu laughed sardonically, but slightly uneasily. He was much stronger than Rupert, and the issue of a fight could not be in doubt. Yet the little dog was keeping his head, coping with the situation.

'You're not exactly a heavyweight, you pansy pom-pom doggy,' said Hargneu. 'I'll give you one chance. Clear off now, or I'll break you in two.'

'Try these for sharpness, you lumbering ponce of a mongrel,' invited Rupert baring his teeth, and he shot a few words of instruction over his shoulder towards the petrified Barthus and Pielet: 'You youngsters, the moment he goes for me, run like hell towards the forest and join up with the old pater and mater.'

'You've asked for it!' roared Hargneu, bracing himself to charge. Yet a certain something held him back. He had just felt on the back of his neck an unfamiliar but very evocative effluvium. Baclin had come through the hedge and gently glided to within a few inches of Hargneu. Since the cur, preoccupied with squaring up to Rupert, had not noticed him, Baclin thought fit to send over a few whiffs of his decidedly devastating breath.

With admirable cunning, Hargneu pretended not to have been affected. Then, with a powerful spring, he threw himself on Baclin. The wolf was prepared. He shifted his head and avoided Hargneu's teeth. Still under the impetus of his charge, the dog dug himself head down in the mud. With a brisk movement Baclin took Hargneu by the neck and was ready to crush the nape.

'Not so fast, Baclin,' said a gruff voice which Rupert found hard to recognize, though he saw that it came from Plantagenet, who had also materialized through the hedge. 'Lay off that get, if it's all t' same to thee. Don't kill him. He's an idiot. He's not so terrible, tha knows.'

There was a burst of wild laughter as yet another shape crashed into the picture, and Grondin speedily covered the two youngsters. All this time Hargneu was near-suffocating with his nose in the mud.

'I'm going to deal with this skiver myself,' thundered Plantagenet in a voice which dumbfounded everyone. 'Let him go, Baclin. Leave him to me.' The wolf loosened his grip. Hargneu fluttered as he tried to stand up. There was hardly time for him to regain his stance. Plantagenet launched one blow with the battering-ram of his head. The dog took off, all four feet in the air, and landed half-stunned. Plantagenet rushed on him, gave him a left and right hook with his snout, then to the stupefaction of everyone he began to make a massive meal of Hargneu's tail. When he had sufficiently mangled that organ he planted his teeth in the fleshiest part that the dog could offer and, with his mouth full, he hissed through Hargneu's piercing shrieks:

'Out of my sight, you sinister shyster. Don't ever let me find you in my path again.'

The dog did not wait to reply. He arched his back to be gone. But now he found himself face to face with Grondin.

'Just a moment,' said the boar calmly. 'Take a good look at me. I am Grondin. The real Grondin. Accept no imitations, though it does seem that Plantagenet, with the aid of a little soot, can put the fear of the lord into you.

'I think,' Grondin continued, 'that from now on Plantagenet can look after himself. But let me warn you that if you are ever tempted even to smell a single hair of him, you

will have me to deal with.' And with a light thrust of his
snout he threw Hargneu into the Guirande. The dog was
borne away on the current, and struck out, shrieking with
terror. He struggled to the far shore and raced towards the
castle, a hairy comet with a flaming tail.

Baclin had a little admiring nod of admiration for Plantagenet who, with great dignity in spite of being black with
mud, came back to salute Rupert. Grondin followed him.

'Ah, Milord,' said the boar. 'I haven't had the pleasure of
your acquaintance before. You have given proof of a courage I had already heard of. My cousin Plantagenet has told
me all about you. I thank you for what you have done for
our children at the risk of your life. I should like to be your
friend. Will you accept?'

'Delighted,' said Rupert. 'And may I thank you in turn for
arriving when you did. I should have taken a fall or two if
I'd wrestled with that blighter.'

'It was a pleasure.'

'Put it there.'

'Chin-chin.'

The dog and the boar exchanged polite sniffs.

'Ah, Baclin!' said Rupert, recognizing Hurlaud's brother
from a previous drawn match. 'Do you come here often?'

'I've never been here before,' said Baclin, somewhat
mystified.

'English humour,' said Rupert. 'Give my regards to
Fulgent when you meet. I must fly. So long, Baclin.'

'Goodnight, milord.'

'So long, Rupert,' said Plantagenet.

'How long?' asked Rupert enigmatically, and he trotted
off into the night.

The little party took the road to Chizé again. By now it
was black night. The two youngsters were tired and clumsy,
but on this night they could do no wrong. The arrival was
triumphant. Hurlaud had painfully risen to welcome them.

Dame Albaine and her children were damp with emotion. Dame Pernale masked everything in a great dither of busyness and came near losing her temper with the refugee authorities for not correctly counting the number of beds required. From all around the forest animals came in to share the communal joy. Plantagenet, who had tolerantly submitted to yet another feast of acorns, was prevailed upon without difficulty to narrate the vicissitudes of the expedition. He stood solid as he spoke, not particularly wishing to sit down. His firm, lively tail swung eloquently from side to side or waved in frenetic windmills according to the stage of the narrative. He came to the instant when he stunned Hargneu with one blow of his head. Suddenly he stopped short and gave a high mezzo-castrato cry. Pielet had just had another nibble at his uncle's fascinating rear.

18

The Return

The days passed calmly and happily. The hospitality of the inhabitants of the forest of Chizé was beyond all praise. The casualties gradually felt their wounds closing and their strength returning, and began to think of home. The owl Uhlan the Wise came three or four times to visit his friends and advise on the situation. He judged it prudent to let some time pass so that the excitement could die down. The game, which had intentionally been spared, was now swarming from Les Combles to Malperthuis. The battue had been totally fruitless. Only Pasquin the badger had been located. But the many galleries he had dug in advance had set men and ferrets completely astray. They had abandoned the earth-stopping they had started, and lost all chance of digging him out. Messire de Frébois and his friends were in a state of deep physical and mental confusion, and the Bishop was on edge that they might abandon the tenets of the Church in favour of Pantheism. Only the Widow Bigotte maintained any consistency, muttering in her corner of the hearth that it was all a trick of the wolves and they would soon be back. Maister Brémand was at his wits' end. He had lost three dogs. Hargneu had lost part of his tail. His daughter Adèle was in a decline, mourning the disappearance of Plantagenet. Hargneu, who was considered responsible for the afflictions visited on the pig, was kept on a very tight leash.

Brousse the magpie had had a complete report from Hargneu and had nearly choked when she heard of Plantagenet's triumph. She knew that she now had not a friend in the forest. Bourcet the sparrow and Lupiot the hedge-rat were very sad in the deserted woods and longed for everyone's return.

So everyone returned.

It was all organized by Hurlaud. But there was none of the urgency of the exodus, with its anguish and uncertainties. The return was a festival, a happy excursion, though carried out with prudence. First a great feast was organized in the forest. All the inhabitants of the woods around were invited. The greatest respect was accorded to the most aged guests. Uhlan the Wise flew over to take the presidential chair. An affecting speech was made by Ferlut de la Tranchée, a great uncle of Baclin and cousin of that Ferlut who had fallen in the line of duty, praising the natural laws which regulated the lives of the animals. Ferlut was himself present at this feast, along with the other departed – Gerdoise, Fulmet, Flambert and Bafrin the Noble. For animals do not possess the faculty to forget.

It was indeed whispered that one day, not long before, one of the first daisies that had pushed through in the meadow of La Ville had been plucked by a tiny grey sparrow and gently placed on a branch of the great old oak near Casse Tombereau where the dead had fallen. That oak is there today, though the willow where Bafrin rested is gone.

After the feast the return was organized with the ferrying of little groups, each gradually and unobtrusively reclaiming possession of their territory.

By the Spring it was all completed. In a forest covert near Stags Crossing Hurlaud, Baclin, Grondin and Plantagenet were gossiping, as males do.

'What are you going to do, Plantagenet? Go back to La Tranchée for a spell, or stay with us?'

'I think I shall be more useful at La Tranchée. At least for a time. I shall be able to learn some vital information from Sobrin and Rupert which might be of use to you.'

'Vital information,' said Grondin with as straight a face as possible.

'And then Mademoiselle Adèle is pining away, it seems. She's a fine young girl, and I haven't the right to make her suffer through sheer selfishness.'

Hurlaud and Baclin began to laugh.

'Ah, that at least is a very good reason. An unselfish reason. A noble reason.'

'That's the path to Pied du Fût.'

'We'll see you, Plantagenet.'

'I'll see you, friends.'

He went away into the undergrowth.

Half an hour later, at twilight, he crossed the porch. Nothing had changed since he had left. Sobrin the donkey saw him first and rushed to meet him.

'Here you are at last! I was giving up hope of ever seeing you again. I have a lot to tell you, old friend.'

The two companions walked together into the courtyard, saying little, in spite of all there was to tell each other.

Maister Brémand, who was coming out at that moment, nearly fell backwards.

'Adèle!' he called. 'Adèle! Quick! Come and see! Plantagenet has come back!'

A slim figure in a white dress flashed from the house and came running towards them.

'Plantagenet!' she cried. 'Plantagenet! My brother, the pig Plantagenet.'

19
'This Is Going To Be Fun'

A working farm is like a ship on a voyage in the deep sea. Its course must always be kept. Its crew can never be wholly idle. But in the rhythm of the farming day, when the cows have been milked and the oxen stalled and fed, there is a time for torpor which can be lifted by the mood of the moment, and the good cheer of a generous master, into an evening of warm and general bliss, sometimes all the more memorable for its not having been anticipated. The return of Plantagenet was not signalled by a formal celebration. That would have been out of place, an inflated incongruity jarring with the measured acceleration of seed and sap and senses towards the high wild carnival of May Day which lay, land-ho, only a short time ahead. But there was a quiet joy of wholesomeness. A wound, though it had been only half-acknowledged, had healed. Plantagenet had come back. La Tranchée was a smoother community. It smiled through the mild night, its lights burned longer, its many voices lowed more contentedly against the ground swell susurration of the green corn growing beyond the walls.

In the days that followed, Adèle spent many hours with Plantagenet. She did not overwhelm him with a great torrent of news, as if to bring him up to date. She seemed to assume

that he had been kept *au courant* with events, wherever he
had been. When she confided in him it was about the
present, her activities, ambitions, affections. The past was
mentioned only by conversational reference, with the im-
plication that nothing needed explaining. It was in this
fashion that she alluded to the herd of pigs, long overdue
in a farm of this capacity, which Maister Brémand had
installed at La Tranchée after Christmas. Plantagenet had,
of course, been aware of them from the moment he returned. They were not housed near him, but in a large sty
at the end of the granaries, and at this season and stage of
their growth they had been given no free access to any
ground outside their confine. To Plantagenet's mind the
newcomers were acutely disturbing, teasels sensitizing his
awareness of status and of mortality to a far too human
degree; for no posy of *plante genet* garlanded their stall, and
no knife would be withdrawn from their throats when the
moment came. But Adèle, though gentle in all her speech,
seemed unembarrassed by the acquisition, and acknowledged no necessity to excuse their presence or their
eventual despatch.

'Is it just that I see more clearly because of my stay in the
forest?' Plantagenet reasoned with himself. 'Is she getting
harder, or am I getting softer? After all, I never knew her to
flinch when the ripe corn was cut, though Grondin himself
suggested that the vegetable truffle might shriek at the moment of passing on to a higher state in his belly. All the
same, there *is* a difference in her, a sense of maturity, a
confidence, a something that seems to *amuse* her.

'And, give the Devil his due,' Plantagenet mused on, 'by
rights, *I'm* the one who should show superior amusement.
I'm the one who knows what really happened at the battue.
Come to that, every animal on the farm knows it too. They
have a secret that the humans can never share. Lack of
communication! The curse of Babel! But it's very con-

venient at the moment. It has saved my skin. I fancy Maister Brémand would not be so cordial if he knew the true facts of the escape of the lords of the forest.'

Brémand had indeed been favouring Plantagenet with far more of his company. In the gloaming pause between labour and supper, when Adèle would sit with Plantagenet, Brémand would join them with Rupert, companionably listening to his daughter, speaking an easy word to his dog and occasionally to Plantagenet, luxuriantly relaxing. The unexpected completion of this band to form a quintet was the presence of the donkey Sobrin, who increasingly showed his unfussy attachment to Plantagenet, and stood warm in the lee, whisking his tail to discourage the flies, an amiable, phlegmatic, totally silent bastion of ease.

When Brémand and Adèle went in to supper and the animals were alone, Plantagenet and Sobrin and Rupert – when he was in the mood to linger and defer his princely titbits – would stay on for the desultory comment and reminiscence of old comrades.

'Life's getting a bit dull,' said Rupert with a yawn one evening. 'Can't we do something?'

'What sort of thing?' asked Sobrin.

'Adventure. Romance. Action.'

'We could band together and do brave deeds,' said Plantagenet. 'Good deeds. With leadership,' he added, with a slight over-inflation of his chest.

'What shall we call ourselves?' asked Sobrin.

'The Three Halberdiers,' said Rupert in a momentary lapse of English militarism.

'*Halberdiers!*' snorted Plantagenet. 'IN to his guts? TWIST in his guts? I couldn't even make sausage-casing out of the ghoulish remnants, and even if I could it's against my basic principles. Where did you go to school? Don't tell me. How about The Three Buccaneers?'

Rupert carefully considered the proposition as if inspecting a suspect bait.

'Where I was at school,' he said, 'the ushers used to predict that when we finally found the New World we should lose our most enterprising characters as piratical adventurers, hiving off to do their own thing and deriving a new name from the verb *boucaner*, to cure meat over a barbecue. Are you sure you chaps in Poitou haven't dreamt up a noun before its time?'

'The Three Muleteers,' said a voice which seemed to come out of the blue, and conveyed an enticing hint of laughter.

'Muleteers? Who said that?' asked Plantagenet. 'Did you, Sobrin?'

'I am *not* a mule,' said Sobrin, with the nearest approach this genial creature could make to outraged dignity.

On another evening there had been a reference to May Day and its Eve, which were almost on them. The festival began before midnight, when the younger people went out into the skirts of the forest with gay music and loud horns, returning after a revel, which was referred to only with the utmost discretion, carrying broken boughs and branches adorned with nosegays and crowns of flowers. Then, in the dawn, the oxen were taken out, garlanded with flowers on their horns, to draw in the may-pole before it was erected, dressed with herbs and flowers and ribbons, for the morning dance. Adèle had mischievously proposed that the procession of oxen should be led by Plantagenet, prinked with sprays of blossom, and she had rushed through the gate to collect daisies, which she brought back to weave into daisy-chains of various lengths, and tried them for size around Plantagenet's neck.

The incident seemed to make Plantagenet depressed and apprehensive.

'I'm worried about Adèle on May-Day Eve,' he said afterwards to Rupert and Sobrin. 'She shouldn't really go out. She doesn't know what it's all about.'

'I can look after myself,' came a voice from the twilight behind them. The three looked round in astonishment and saw Adèle. She moved towards them, smiling, rounded the group and faced the translucent green of the fading sky.

'Because I look with love on friend and foe, and victim and deceiver,' she said, 'and praise my Lord for all his creatures, I'm not *thick*. I know this world. I know myself. I know my Lord. Do you think every loving maiden has to be a *foolish* virgin?'

Plantagenet was gazing at her in utter amazement.

'You spoke!' he said.

'Of course I spoke.'

'But I didn't see your lips move.'

'I'm not a ventriloquist. Do *your* lips always move when you speak? You speak as fluently as you think.'

'But you spoke our language.'

'I got tired of waiting until you spoke mine. In any case, because of muscular changes in the pharynx, which derive from Man's standing upright on two legs, you never will.'

'You spoke our language!' Plantagenet repeated. 'And you understand it. So that was the change. That was why you sounded so superior.'

'Superior?'

'*Amused*,' Plantagenet hastily corrected himself. 'I knew you were different. You were mature. You were confident. Isn't that just what I said?' Plantagenet desperately appealed to Rupert and Sobrin. They confusedly agreed, though they had no recollection of any such comment from Plantagenet.

'I'm not superior. I'm equal,' said Adèle. 'I'm one of the boys. . . . One of creation,' she added in a hurried amendment. 'Male and female created He them and without Him was made nothing that was made.'

'What shall we do?' she asked. 'Adventure? Romance? Have you room for a Sweetheart of the Company among the Three Muleteers?'

'This,' said Plantagenet with emphasis, 'this is going to be *fun*.'

HALIC: THE STORY OF A GREY SEAL

Ewan Clarkson

'He was born on the running tide. The sea and the rain cleaned him, the wind dried him, and the sun-hot stones warmed his body. He was an Atlantic grey seal, and his name was Halic.'

But Halic's mother does not nurse him for long. Two weeks later a storm separates them and washes the young seal away from his home beach.

Alone in a pitiless environment, Halic must learn to defend himself against the predators that threaten his life.

'Danger from killer whales, sharks and man . . . a vividness that will appeal to every reader.'

Irish Times

£1.00

FORTUNE'S WHEEL

Rhoda Edwards

1469: the Wars of the Roses are raging. Young Richard Gloucester stands in the wings, witnessing the formidable struggle for power between his brother, Edward IV, and the magnificent Warwick – the Kingmaker.

But Richard's own life is in turmoil, for he has fallen in love with Anne – Warwick's daughter. Now he is torn by a bitter conflict: his loyalties divided between the passion he feels for his enemy's child and a fierce loyalty to his brother.

Fortunes change with violent and dizzying speed – from triumph and power to poverty and despair, culminating in the two bloody battles which resolve Edward and Warwick's argument. It seems that at last Richard and Anne can be together – but even now their happiness is threatened . . .

'Her interpretative flair and accurate descriptive detail put her head and shoulders above the rest of the field' *Times Literary Supplement*

£1.00

SOME OF OUR BEST FRIENDS ARE ANIMALS

Peter Spence

Life at Cricket St Thomas was never quite the same after the Taylor family converted the house and grounds into a wildlife park. Some very unusual animal personalities made their mark. Like Twiggy the elephant, or the barnacle goose who fell in love with a red deer – not to mention the sealion who hijacked a Range Rover.

'Life among the residents of a wildlife park seems to have all the ingredients of the Marx Brothers joining the Goons in an unscripted farce down on the farm'
Coventry Evening Telegraph

85p

BESTSELLERS FROM ARROW

All these books are available from your bookshop or newsagent or you can order them direct. Just tick the titles you want and complete the form below.

A CHOICE OF CATASTROPHIES	Isaac Asimov	£1.95
BRUACH BLEND	Lillian Beckwith	95p
THE HISTORY MAN	Malcolm Bradbury	£1.60
A LITTLE ZIT ON THE SIDE	Jasper Carrott	£1.25
EENY MEENY MINEY MOLE	Marcel A'Agneau	£1.50
HERO	Leslie Deane	£1.75
TRAVELS WITH FORTUNE	Christine Dodwell	£1.50
11th ARROW BOOK OF CROSSWORDS	Frank Henchard	95p
THE LOW CALORIE MENU BOOK	Joyce Hughes	90p
THE PALMISTRY OF LOVE	David Brandon-Jones	£1.50
DEATH DREAMS	William Katz	£1.25
PASSAGE TO MUTINY	Alexander Kent	£1.50
HEARTSOUNDS	Marth Weinman Lear	£1.75
LOOSELY ENGAGED	Christopher Matthew	£1.25
HARLOT	Margaret Pemberton	£1.60
TALES FROM A LONG ROOM	Peter Tinniswood	£1.50
INCIDENT ON ATH	E. C. Tubb	£1.15
THE SECOND LADY	Irving Wallace	£1.75
STAND BY YOUR MAN	Tammy Wynette	£1.75
DEATH ON ACCOUNT	Margaret Yorke	£1.00
	Postage	
	Total	

ARROW BOOKS, BOOKSERVICE BY POST, PO BOX 29, DOUGLAS, ISLE OF MAN, BRITISH ISLES

Please enclose a cheque or postal order made out to Arrow Books Limited for the amount due including 10p per book for postage and packing for orders within the UK and 12p for overseas orders.

Please print clearly

NAME ....

ADDRESS...

....

Whilst every effort is made to keep prices down and to keep popular books in print, Arrow Books cannot guarantee that prices will be the same as those advertised here or that the books will be available.